Young Man,
I Think You're Dying

JOAN FLEMING

DOVER PUBLICATIONS, INC.
Mineola, New York

Bibliographical Note
This Dover edition, first published in 2018, is an unabridged republication
of the work originally published by John Curley & Associates, London, in 1970.

Library of Congress Cataloging-in-Publication Data
Names: Fleming, Joan, 1908–1980, author.
Title: Young man, I think you're dying / Joan Fleming.
Description: Dover edition. | Mineola, New York : Dover Publications, Inc.,
   [2018] | This Dover edition, first published in 2018, is an unabridged republication of the work
   originally published by John Curley & Associates, London, in 1970.
Identifiers: LCCN 2017047953 | ISBN 9780486822976 (print) | ISBN 0486822974 (print)
Classification: LCC PR6011.L46 Y68 2018 | DDC 823/.914—dc23
LC record available at https://lccn.loc.gov/2017047953

Manufactured in the United States by LSC Communications
82297401   2018
www.doverpublications.com

Young Man,
I Think You're Dying

"So slowly, slowly rase she up
And slowly came she nigh him,
And when she drew the curtains by —
'Young man, I think you're dying.'

'Farewell,' she said, 'ye virgins all
And shun the fault I fell in:
Henceforth take warning by the fall
of cruel Barbara Allen.' "

—Lowland Scottish Ballad

CHAPTER I

Pizzas! He adjusted his expression to one of disgust and contempt, but lovingly, in the manner of an artist, he picked up the sliced onion and arranged it down the pastry in a straight professional line next to the sliced tomato. Far back, out of sight, in his utmost mind, he loved them; the smell was, to him, entirely felicitous and it was not possible to be unhappy in an atmosphere of such sensual content.

However, in his social set work was an evil thing, something to be avoided if humanly possible; a nuisance, a drag, a bore, something that had to be put up with, like parents, until such time as one could escape to *freedom*. For a long time, anyway until he was fifteen, Joe had not known the meaning of the much-used word *freedom*—until he looked it up in a dictionary which his poor father used for crossword puzzles. It was faintly disappointing to find that this golden, glittering word which he had used liberally for so long simply meant personal liberty, non-slavery, but he had swallowed it along with the vitamin pills his mother pressed on him every morning.

Now, after working for two years for Silas d'Ambrose (he insisted on the apostrophe, he himself always making it audible) he fully realised that he was, indeed, a victim of slavery and that freedom meant having your own business, sitting with your feet up on one of the tables reading *Playboy*, issuing occasional reminders such as: "Have you washed your hands, Joe?" "Mind you cut the bad bits off those tomatoes!" whilst your employees slaved and slaved.

The pizza bar in which he slaved was in a house in a small eighteenth-century street in Soho, due shortly for demolition. In the flat above the bar Madame Joan, Palmist, carried on her trade. A few doors down, a shop selling rubber goods and medicines for waning sexual prowess bore the stone words on the grey brick wall above the ground floor window: EXCHANGE AND BULLION MART and the date 1721. There had been a crumbling notice above the pizza bar, which Silas had had taken down to make way for the word PIZZAS in bright blue neon electric lettering; it now hung indoors for the amusement of customers and read: M. SLY CORSETIERE. Joe personally had no time for these kind of jokes; his own place, when he had it, would be the last word in modernity; it would have a Ladies as well as a Gents and there would be Dames and Messieurs over the doors, such as had impressed him deeply at London Air Terminus. He would not have the huge gas ovens and the slaves working behind a counter in full view of the customers, but conceal the business side behind a tasteful modern stained-glass partition; gorgeous naked girls with huge bosoms would glide in and out from behind the screens bearing plates of pizzas; or nearly naked, like the girls at the Playboy Club. He would insist that they disappear behind the screen as soon as they had served the food; this vanishing would titillate the customer so that he wouldn't get bored staring at them for too long. Joe had a small notebook in which, when he had time, he jotted down his own "*Do It Yourself Market Research*," under the simple heading *Plans*, keeping the book carefully locked away from his mother who, if she had found it, would have read it aloud to his father to the accompaniment of the giggling that annoyed him so much.

It was not fashionable to like your boss and when he was with his chums Joe would be as loud as the others in protests of detestation but, in fact, his liking for Silas went beyond a mere sneaking approval. He admired him very much; his ease of manner, his good temper and, best of all, the way he paid promptly, with the occasional reminder: "And don't forget I've paid the Income Tax."

He was kind to Joe, too. When, for instance, Joe had given him a false name because he was so deeply ashamed of his own name, Silas had discovered it over the question of National Insurance and had said: "So you're really called Joe Bogey, are you? I say, I *say*! With or without the *e*? I'd keep the *e* if I were you; like me, you're descended from the Huguenots, who were immigrants to this blasted sceptered isle."

"Oh yes?" Joe had said, looking his most gormless because he did not approve of classy language.

"We fled from oppression in France in the eighteenth century. Your name would probably have been *de la Bougerie* or something of the kind that the poor English clots couldn't wrap their tongues round. So you hang on to your *e*. And when you give your name don't stutter and go red and stand on one leg; say boldly and clearly Joseph Bogey, *with an e.* That'll shut them up! They used to call Napoleon Buonaparte Boney, so you have an honourable precedent and don't forget it."

For two years and more Joe had observed Silas and all his ways; disapproval and bewilderment had gradually changed to admiration. As he grew up along with his playmates who, with the passage of time, had become verbose and revolutionary, he was given to understand that his boss was someone to be despised, a member of the privileged class and thus never to be trusted; Joe did trust him all the same and looked up to him as a do-er of the Right Thing.

Even over the vexed question of length of hair Joe had, after a pretty tight struggle, meekly given in and in due course his chums had accepted his short hair as part of the slavery with which they themselves would not put up.

Silas had clapped the tall white chef's hat over his long, greasy brown locks and dragged him over to a looking-glass. He had laughed: "You look a right Charlie, don't you?" The glance Joe had given himself was subliminal, a full moment of viewing would have been too horrifying, he had snatched off the starched hat and held it in front of him as though he were about to be sick into it.

"You see, long hair's all right if you're a bricklayer's mate and don't mind mortar in your hair, or if you're a Council's employee, bashing holes in the road and like your hair smelling of drains. But here my customers don't want your hairs in their pizzas. Get me? So it's either becoming an expert chef with short hair and a big future before you, or joining your chums with plenty of hair but no prospects. You can take it or leave it."

And with the heart-warming smell of pizzas in his head and eighteen pounds a week in prospect it had seemed worth a searing visit to the barber and an acute draught round his ears for a few hours afterward.

There were two of them working in the bar, Joe being the senior boy, and they worked on a rota; one week from six p.m. to midnight and the next week a visit to the bar at six a.m. to make the dough and leave it to rise, then a return to the bar and work from twelve to three, with both of them there on a Saturday night. Two extremely plain girls did the washing up, especially chosen for their looks and figures which were unattractive beyond belief, and a very superior person indeed, called Mrs. James Trelawny, mopped the floors and wiped the Formica table tops and plastic chair seats. Silas appeared to do nothing whatever, lounging elegantly about, smoking Balkan Sobranies but making quite sure that no customer left the bar without paying him.

Like small blessings Joe dropped tiny fragments of margarine over the whole colourful tray he had now prepared with mushroom slices, tomatoes, aubergine slivers, onion, cheese, a criss-cross of anchovy fillets, and oregano herb, finely chopped and sprinkled over the whole. He opened the door of the second oven, felt the temperature with his hand, careful not to touch the hot metal, swung the heavy tray on to his shoulder and with a flourish which he had achieved only in the course of time, slid the whole into the black depths and swung the door closed. In the same operation he brought out the sizzling contents from No. 1 oven, laying it down in all its fragrant glory.

"That's a clever boy, give us one!" The high husky voice was only too familiar, it was a red-head called W. Sledge of whom Joe had stood in some awe since he had come to live in the same tower block and share the same play-ground when they were both ten. It annoyed him that W. Sledge should have turned up on a Monday night, their not so busy time; the time made it much more difficult to give him a free meal.

"Eff off!" he said, sliding a pizza on to a plate with a large metal slice and placing it on the glass shelf for the customer to pick up.

"Don't be like that! It's important."

"It would be," Joe returned sarcastically as he slid another three-and sixpennyworth on to a plate.

W. Sledge folded his arms and leaned gracefully against the wall, watching his toiling friend with faint jeering amusement. Though he was not to know it, he bore a strong resemblance to the young Shelley with unhealthy pale features of rat-like proportions and a wild cacophony of tangled red hair; he was wearing skin-tight pants, an orange-coloured polo necked shirt over which was a fisher-man's knit V-necked sweater, the tasteful ensemble finished by several rows of beads which appeared to be made of date stones or something and smelled strongly of the Middle East.

He was extremely picturesque and added lustre to the otherwise fairly drab crowd of customers in the pizza bar. Silas, however, gave him a beady look and said: "Can we help you, sir?" though he knew him perfectly well by sight. This meant all too clearly: you-better-bloody-well-sit-down-and-behave-yourself and was by no means unjustified, as it was W. Sledge's tendency to come in with a crowd of rowdies and there were occasionally symptoms of an inclination to break the place up. But tonight, because he wished urgently to communicate with his friend Joe, he sat down meekly and accepted the plate of hot savoury pizza which Silas banged down in front of him, together with the implements for eating it, suavely wrapped in a folded paper napkin as though they were rather indecent things, which they were not. His behaviour, in fact, was impeccable; when he had finished eating he threw one arm over the back of his chair and sat staring meaningfully at his friend, picking his teeth until the stroke of midnight, after which not another pizza was served and the unused ones were put under a plastic cover for the next day.

Joe was hustled along the overcrowded pavements through the usual cosmopolitan crowd jostling and struggling nowhere; outside Bob's Baked Potato Bar, which in the dark backward and abysm of time had been the best restaurant in London, an elderly couple stood and shivered miserably, bitterly disappointed in the meal they had had.

"It must have changed hands, dear," the old lady was murmuring to her husband as he beckoned a cab. But W. Sledge, too, hailed the taxi and as it drew up he snatched at the handle and pushed Joe inside whilst at the same time firmly pressing the old gentleman back on to the pavement with the sole of his foot stretched out backwards so that the taxi driver could not see it.

"He kicked you!" the old lady said indignantly.

W. Sledge slammed the taxi door and leaned forward to him through the driver's small glass aperture: "Fiery Beacon!"

The taxi lurched off down the Haymarket and the old gentleman said: "He didn't really kick me, dear. He pushed me with his foot to be exact, but it hurts rather."

But though W. Sledge had whipped up a potential event it was, in fact, disappointing in that Joe knew in advance what was expected of him. It was his turn.

It would seem that only two alternatives had presented themselves to the young Sledge in the way of a career, the first and obvious one being that of entertainer, but he had found to his chagrin that time, in respect of the beat, meant nothing at all to him. Though he was able to bang drums with great energy and enthusiasm he unfortunately always banged them at the wrong split second. Several groups had given him a trial but he had been turned down by them all. He had to face the sad fact that he was not "musical." So there had been no alternative but for him to become what is called an *entrepreneur*. This word at one time applied to someone who, for instance, ran a pierrot show on some seaside pier but it has been upgraded with time and now applies simply to an organiser working for himself. W. Sledge became an organiser in that he organised himself into obtaining goods without payment and selling them at various sources of which he kept a record in a notebook, written in a code which he had invented himself. In the course of time these activities advanced, if the word is relevant, from the category of Petty Crime to that of Crime. In the same way the appellation Petty Thief advanced into Thief but since that word has been devalued W. Sledge settled for *entrepreneur* finding it more interesting than the ambiguous alternative: Company Director.

By sheer prestidigitation, details of which would make a useful handbook in itself for those wishing to imitate, W. Sledge had, at the age of twenty-one, achieved a pleasant flat of his own in the council tower block in which he had lived with his parents since he was ten. He had kept a beautiful Hindu mistress of fourteen whom he rented to other *entrepreneurs*, strictly during the day. He received unemployment benefit. He had achieved a six-year-old Jaguar which he kept in an underground garage in return for serving petrol during the early hours of the morning every other weekend when not on the parking lot by Fiery Beacon. He was also a chairman and founding member of an exclusive club with the name of The Wotchas, the membership of which never exceeded six, a brotherhood not in the least resembling but almost as closely knit as the Freemasons. Absolute loyalty was the prerequisite of this club, the joke name being the exact reason for its existence in that they were actually watchers one for another. Ten per cent, the watcher received.

This brief summing-up of W. Sledge's career makes sad reading: he had achieved too much, too soon. An infant until his last birthday in the eyes of the law, he considered he "had everything."

"It's an old lady in Kensington, W8," W. Sledge said as they sat back in the cab. "It's an absolute cinch since I cleaned the windows there last week and I know my way around."

"No, no, I wouldn't touch it. I wouldn't like an old lady to get hurt," Joe returned firmly.

"There's no question of her getting hurt," W. Sledge reproved. "Not much, anyway."

"Aw, Sledgey." Joe sighed at the wickedness of it. He also used the affectionate term because none of his acquaintances was allowed to use the so-called Christian name by which he had evidently been christened: it stank. "Why pick on me?"

"It's your time round. What's up with you anyway? Getting goose flesh?"

In an attempt to change the subject Joe asked what he thought he was up to, joining a window-cleaning firm; that was a corny old game, only fit for an elderly lag, and it meant giving up the Social Security loot.

Sledge smiled that smile he used when he was feeling the utmost superiority to the dim wit with whom he was conversing.

"Oh my dear!" He winced at the pain the remark caused him.

"Well, I mean to say   are you slippin', joinin' a firm? You must be off your top."

W. Sledge brought a pair of large dark glasses out of his hip pocket and put them on before he turned to stare at Joe, whose face was only intermittently lit as the taxi slipped past the Houses of Parliament and along to the Embankment. He was dissatisfied with his eyes which, he realised, were not compelling enough, in fact they were not compelling at all, they were shallow and poky and pale, and as he lived with a girl who had compelling dark eyes of the saucer variety he was extremely conscious of this deficiency in himself, so when he wished to be forceful he resorted to the artificiality of black dark glasses of an abnormal size.

"Who said anything about joining a firm? Haven't you any wits at all, man?" He sighed heavily at the ennui of having to explain anything so simple. "You only need a short ladder, little more than a pair of steps; a water-proof jacket out of which there's a washleather hanging, a cloth cap ..." he stopped to cackle with laughter at the idea of himself in a cloth cap ...

"Right? You park the Jag a little way off one of these old-fashioned great big blocks of flats. You must make sure it's Kensington, though, because there's sure to be at least one *Lady* something, if not three or four, in the block. You take a note of one name on the name plates in the entrance so that if there's a porter, there nearly always is but they're usually in their own pads, sitting in front of their fires watching telly; if there's a porter snoopin' around you tell him you're going up to Lady So-and-so's. If not, you start off up the stairs; you stump up and down, round and round and sooner or later, man, some dear old lady sees you and squeaks: 'A window cleaner! Just what I want,' and asks you how much you charge. Well, you think of the lowest figure and halve it . . ."

He almost, not quite, yawned at the simplicity of it all. "Well, I mean, you're inside . . . it's peanuts. Mind you, she's not as green as she's cabbage-looking, she never leaves you alone in the room, but she stands there smiling whilst you're having a good dekko and she's watching the marvellous shiny job you're making of the windows. She's always pleased with your work, maybe there's a cuppa at the end of it or maybe a tip. She'll always ask for your card and when you haven't got one on you, she'll write down your address so she can get in touch with you next time she wants her windows cleaned . . ."

They had arrived at Fiery Beacon. "Which entrance?" the cabby shouted over his shoulder.

"South." W. Sledge gave him a five-shilling tip and the cabby grinned conspiratorially before driving off. Chaps like Sledge were always his best customers.

It was drizzling slightly but with one accord they crossed over the road and leaned against the railings, staring down into the great, grey-green, greasy river, sliding evilly seawards.

"In other words," Joe said, becoming a trifle cynical because he knew his Sledge, "in other words, you've done it exactly once."

"Now, now!" Sledge reproved.

"Once," Joe repeated firmly.

"What are you going on about?" Sledge asked. "It's not a crime."

"Not yet it isn't, not yet." And then Joe suddenly and angrily shouted: "Not yet!" and his voice, tiny and ineffectual, was carried off like a fragment of paper on the surface of the swollen river.

Being able to see practically nothing, W. Sledge took off his glasses and put them back into his pocket. He leaned, back to the railings, and ignored the river. He looked at his home, his refuge, his pad, a twenty-two story block of flats in which he lived a double life. It never ceased to amuse him that he could live his own life as householder, and brothel-keeper on the side, within a hundred air, not square, *air* yards of his far from loving parents who firmly believed that he shared a bachelor flat with friends in Colindale. He thought it immensely clever that he should be the tenant of the council under the name of S. Ledge. He could have thought up any number of names but the near-danger of the S. Ledge gave him immense pleasure. Number 40: Mr. and Mrs. Frank Sledge. Number 102: Mr. S. Ledge.

It was, in fact, less risky than even he thought, life itself continually offering far more coincidences than fiction, such as the announcement in the obituary column of *The Times* of the deaths on the same day of two unrelated people called, for instance, Kipper.

The tower block carried the name of Fiery Beacon after the public house on the site on which it was partly built. The old cracked wooden sign which had swung outside the public house for two or three hundred years now hung in the council chamber, an imaginative gesture on the part of a council chairman. Before the public house there had, in fact, been a fiery beacon, lighted when there was a fog, to warn river shipping of an obstacle of sorts which had long since been removed.

Only sometimes, in certain kinds of weather and when the sun hung low over the river on a still, still evening, did it remotely resemble a fiery beacon from some distance away. At present, late at night it was an imaginary tower of the "young-Roland-to-the-dark-tower-came" kind of tower, immensely tall and immensely black, with only here and there a lighted window, pinkish, bluish or yellowish, shining through the unlined curtains. It was most people's bedtime.

But Joe knew with a depressed certainty that it was by no means his bedtime, he knew as sure as God made little apples that he would have to do what was required of him before he went to bed because it was His Turn, and he was bound to obey. He was only thankful that he was on a late rota. This week he was not the early-morning pastry maker in the pizza bar. Talk about slavery, he thought, there'll always be slavery. He couldn't formulate his opinion exactly but he meant that there would always be people who were in thrall to other people, no matter how much humanity might progress. He had watched for W. Sledge too often to be able to back out of his commitments now; W. Sledge had only to go along to the police and give Joe's name for him to be, at the very least, put on probation instantly because of past affairs. He did not want to be on probation because he had a steady job now which, though he never admitted it, he much enjoyed, and because his boss would, he thought, sack him.

He wondered wearily just how long this thraldom would last; would he still be dogsbodying for W. Sledge when he was a middle-aged man with his own thriving business and streamlined Jaguar; a much newer model than that of W. Sledge? He said humbly:

"Well, this one and that's it."

"How do you mean?" W. Sledge snapped.

"You know damn' well how I mean. I'm thinking of retiring."

"From The Wotchas?"

"Um."

W. Sledge allowed a stream of abuse to slip out between his lips as smoothly and darkly as the river flowing below but it didn't mean anything much and he did it automatically, without thinking what he was actually saying. He was planning. He was one who preferred to take it easy, he liked a spot of luxury, not for him the petty thief's breathless escape from the screws, running along the top of long Kensington brick walls leading to cul-de-sacs, in his plimsolls, then flattening himself against huge black wet tree trunks trying to avoid the sweep of their powerful hand lamps.

He liked to have his car as near as possible to the job, with his chauffeur sitting patiently waiting to start off the instant he was safely inside. Besides, a car AND chauffeur was not an object of suspicion as a rule.

He drew in his surplus saliva with a long-drawn-out hiss. "This job is easy, dead easy, man. There's nothink to it. First floor apartment, flat roof jutting out at the back, a room built on years ago, studio or something, with a skylight, man, with a skylight!" He did a few tap-dancing steps to show his pleasure. "The ladder's hid in the shrubbery, and what a shrubbery, filthy! And as the ladder was nicked from a regular window cleaner and has his name stencilled on the side, it won't do no harm when found leaning against the wall where I'll leave it. And guess what?"

Joe couldn't guess what, nor did he try.

"There's one of these here old-fashioned tables inside the flat, you follow? Glass-topped with treasure within, sheltering from the day-to-day dust."

"Treasure?"

"Snuff-boxes, man, and other small hallmarked objects, *aye-twee*, they call them. This old girl's dad or husband must have collected them and does she treasure them! Not that I had time to examine them!" He laughed raucously, "But I've examined others, spread out for all to see in the windows and showcases of the Bond Street dealers, *Old* Bond Street I should say. And in the big sale-rooms, Sotheby's and Christie's, for example, you can look at them close, handle them. There's a chap watching you to see you don't nick them mind, but you can look till your eyes fall out, there's no harm in looking now, is there? So I know what old silver looks like, all right. I should do, by now. It's not shiny, like new. Soft, it is, looks more like the old tins we used to have around except it's never rusty. Tin," he mused thoughtfully. "I've got so's I can recognise it at a glance, I don't have to squint about for the hallmark, I can see for myself what's silver and what isn't. Phew ... uhu ... Christ in spats! These snuff-boxes, I reckon there's not a dud amongst the lot." Somewhere about his person he found a toothpick and started to use it liberally, removing the morsels left from the pizza he had consumed a short time ago and for which he had had to pay before leaving. "Silly old trout!" he mused.

Joe leaned against the railings, holding his head in his hands, elbows on the chilly iron. He wished very much he was in bed.

"Come on, buck up, JoBo, man. The Jag's over there, in the car park, petrol in, tyres okay."

"You're not going like that, I hope," Joe fervently hoped. The rattle of his beads alone would waken the dead.

"I'm wearing my Aquascutum," he said in an excruciatingly refined voice, "buttoned up to the neck, plenty of room in the pockets. One, just one of those snuff-boxes will fetch fifty, couldn't fetch less. There is around a dozen at a rough guess so if I take four in each pocket, and have the goodness to leave her two, I'll have four hundred quid or so at best," he smiled slyly, "enough to keep you and me for a couple of weeks, eh JoBo?" He added hastily, "I don't mean that I'm halving it, don't get me wrong, but twenty per cent for you tonight, Jobo, just for a treat, eh?"

In the heart of darkest Kensington, not now so very dark because it was lit by blinding neon lighting which replaced the old hanging brackets but made it difficult to see anything at all clearly, the block of flats was red brick and the entrance was a baroque stone canopy over double half-glass swing doors. Large letters on one of the stone pillars proclaimed the numbers 1–30.

The Jaguar, driven by a young chauffeur in a peaked cap, slid to a stop; it was five minutes to one a.m.

"She'll wake up, of course, unless she's doped herself with the sleeping tablets the doctor's given her, like a lot of these old things do, nowadays. But sure enough she'll sleep with her bedroom door locked and if she hears anything she'll put her head under the bedclothes and pray."

"And what?"

"Pray!"

"You'd better watch it," Joe murmured sullenly, "you're too bloody confident, if you ask me, too cocky by a long chalk."

Mr. W. Sledge was pulling on expensive, well-fitting black antelope gloves from a Jermyn Street glovers. "Yew-man nature is what you've got to study," he advised, "you can't get nowhere if you don't *know how people tick*," he hissed into Joe's actual earhole so, for the moment, Joe was engaged in cleaning out his earhole and omitted to wish him luck. Sledge vanished, not through the entrance door which would, at that time of night, be locked, but between the building and the surrounding hedge and, presumably, round the back.

Joe took off the chauffeur's cap which he had worn before without knowing that the "badge" on the front was a coronet and that Sledge had "acquired" it from the chauffeur of a peer-of-the-realm in a public house not far from the House of Lords. He examined the greasy mark on the lining, as he had done before, and found that others must have worn it, because last time he used it, it had resembled the map of Ireland but was becoming more shapeless with the passage of time.

Ireland . . . his mother was at present there, at a little town in the south called Ballyhoola where her son-in-law was a vet, and she was due back at any moment. She had been attending the birth of her first grandchild, which had unexpectedly turned out to be two, thus prolonging her visit.

"Uncle Joe!" he said aloud to try the sound, "Uncle Joe!"

He was completely relaxed, one of the attractions of the friendship of
W. Sledge was that he inspired confidence and freedom from constraint
in his employees. Joe felt rather less tension than the wearer of the peaked
hat might have felt were he waiting for the peer-of-the-realm to come
out of the dentist, much less, in fact, because the peer's chauffeur would
have been worried about such things as meters and meter-wardens.

He did not, as anyone in a state of even mild anxiety might have done,
follow W. Sledge in his mind:

(1) The slipping round the back: 1 minute.
(2) Finding the ladder and putting it into position, ½ minute.
(3) Climbing ladder, 6 seconds.
(4) Covering small area on skylight with coating of putty, ½ minute.
(5) Pressing glass till it broke and picking out as much as possible
    without letting any fall inside, if poss., 1 minute.
(6) Gripping bar, opening skylight wide enough for entry, getting
    in, ½ minute at most.
(7) Dropping lightly down, making bee-line for living-room,
    unlocking living-room door (always locked on hall side by old
    ladies living alone), closing it, pressing-in glass on table top
    with cushion. Bringing fountain pen size torch out of pocket
    to illuminate snuff-boxes, 1 minute.
(8) Picking snuff-boxes out from amongst bits of broken glass,
    2 minutes if selective.
(9) Looking round to see if anything left in the way of identification
    (as if there could be!), split second.
(10) Nipping out at the speed of sound, closing front door of flat
    quietly with the utmost caution, 2 seconds.
(11) Descending stairs, 10 seconds.
(12) Coping with inside main door catches, 10 seconds.
(13) Shutting front door quietly.

Operation complete in ten minutes and Bob's your uncle.

It was a quarter-of-an-hour, in fact, but Joe was so interested in the
new idea of being an uncle that though he had the engine running for
a good eight minutes he had not even begun to wonder if anything

had gone wrong when W. Sledge reappeared. He started off even before Sledge had shut the door with a quiet clunk.

"I'm an uncle, I forgot to tell you," he said chattily, as they moved off: "I've twin nieces; they're Irish, my sister married a vet who's a marvellous jockey, beat that! He's an Irish amateur, came over for the Grand National. But two nieces at once—eh?"

"Shut up about your effing relations . . ."

Startled, Joe glanced sideways at his friend W. Sledge, who had lost his usual fairly good-natured aplomb and was being sick through his gloved fingers and on to the rubber mat between his feet, splashing vilely his pointed-toed, elastic-sided boots. Alarmed now, Joe stopped the car and stared helplessly at the mess.

He began to feel rather ill himself, there were sensations such as he had never experienced in the region of his heart, not so much a pain as certain jiggings about which had the effect of making him breathless. He became slightly dizzy, his mouth dried up, he began to shiver. He felt as he might have done if he had arrived in another country, travelling in something much faster than the Concorde; he had arrived conscious but with nothing but fear, the horrible metallic taste of fear in his mouth.

"You've killed her!" He knew suddenly all about the fragility of old ladies, how easily they died, how easily anyone died, in fact, if they were subjected to too great physical stress. How vile, how vile it was, he realised, to manhandle an old lady, like playing catch-as-catch-can with a piece of valuable china. How stupid, how senseless, how absolutely non-okay.

He knew all about Sledge's violent temper too, about how he sometimes tortured cats. He was wise, suddenly he knew and felt everything with a kind of uncanny out-of-this-world sensitivity. In your ordinary senses you would never kill an old lady, not unless you were a monster of sorts, but fear might make you, fear of being caught, like animal fear on the edge of being trapped.

He thought of Silas d'Ambrose and the contempt his boss would have of anything botched so disgustingly; he could see the expression on his face, that fastidious repugnance.

He thought of how he ought to have warned W. Sledge: "Don't do the old lady any harm!" he might have said, but how out-of-tune it would have been, how gauche, clumsy and not okay at all; Sledge would have jeered at any such advice from Joe. "What do you take me for, a thug?" he might have said: "Come off it!"

"What are you stopping for?" Sledge grumbled.

There was nothing he wished to say, no comment he could make aloud; he put the car into gear and slid away from the kerb; for a moment he could not remember where they were and drove mindlessly forward but soon he had to stop at the busy, winding Kensington Church Street, and remembered. He turned south and drove slowly and carefully back home. On the rough ground where the Fiery Beacon's cars were parked he stopped, took off his chauffeur's cap and stowed it away under the seat. He turned and looked at his companion; their faces were greenish in the neon lighting. W. Sledge jerked his head, meaning "get out," and this Joe did. He stood watching Sledge struggling over the gear-lever into the driving seat. He thought: Surely he's not going to drive off without a word?

No, he wasn't; he rolled down the window, his face near Joe's: he looked ghastly. He said: "Be seein' you," and drove off. Never in Joe's experience had W. Sledge said less.

CHAPTER II

Joe's father, when Joe was at the age of nine, from being a fine footballer (playing half-back for Fulham football team one year) had become an immobile mass of flesh, a victim of multiple sclerosis which had started in a small way but spread with alarming speed so that in a matter of weeks he was unable to use his legs and then his arms. He had spent months in hospitals and had had every new form of treatment tried upon him until finally he had settled for living at home and being looked after by his family, helped by relays of home helps and district nurses. From their tiny house in a part of Chelsea which had since become smart, they were allocated a fine, almost penthouse, flat in the new tower block beside the river towards Battersea. There, by the window, on the twenty-first and top floor, his father would sit all day in the wheel chair in which he could not even propel himself into another room. There was still some movement in his hands and lower arms, and he was able to do crossword puzzles, play chess and read the papers, to feed himself (just) and to turn the radio on and off. Two nurses came at night to put him to bed and again in the morning to get him up, to wash and dress him and lift him about.

His wife was a part-time assistant in a department store within easy walking distance and on weekday mornings the meals-on-wheels service would bring hot food for the invalid. It would seem that on the whole he found life worth living, he took a keen interest in the doings of his family, would listen eagerly for his wife's return from work, would comment in a lively manner on the day's events, however minute, and never grumbled about his condition.

His family, wife, son and daughter would store up the day's tiny happenings and relate them when they came home. He had, for instance, been immensely pleased when Joe had repeated the conversation he had had with his boss regarding his Huguenot origins, it had kept his father happy and chuckling for days. It is possible that the continued presence of this tragedy endowed the family with a certain kindness and concern for others that they might not otherwise have had.

Thus it was not out of character that Joe, as he ascended in the lift, should begin to worry about his father. There were so many things that had had to be explained to him, pizzas, for instance, because they were unknown in England about the time his father became immobile.

But there was, too, a great deal that he did not tell his father: W. Sledge and The Wotchas, for instance, had been expurgated entirely. But if there was anything amiss his father, whose powers of observation had been, possibly, sharpened by his condition, would be sure to ask if anything was wrong. He would notice if Joe was starting a cold, had lipstick on his face, smelt of drink, had been in a fight. Similarly if there was any particular elation about him his father would not fail to notice and make some kind of comment. He wasn't inquisitive but he had this very natural desire to participate in the lives of his family.

So when the lift stopped at the twenty-first floor Joe did not get out but sent it sliding up to the next floor, which was the top and far from being a delightful flat roof from which one could survey London from end to end, it was cluttered up with all kinds of utility objects, such as water tanks and sheds covering the vital parts of the lift machinery. Furthermore, none of the inhabitants were allowed up there. On the other hand, there was no satisfactory way of stopping them, someone would have been killed in the attempt to climb to the top if there hadn't been reasonable access.

All the same, amazingly few people seemed to want to use the roof top and Joe had a corner where he kept an upturned apple box on which he could sit and meditate on the mutability of mundane affairs, or merely pick his teeth. This was the sort of time when it was essential to be alone, to assess his situation and decide what he was going to do about it.

He could shout and rant and talk incessantly about freedom and the bloody awfulness of adults with his friends; in his spare time he could revolutionise, tear down road signs, have a go at taking pot, wreck telephone boxes, help others to steal, kick policemen during riots, allow himself to look extremely dirty and untidy, have sex all over the place, but it was a drag. It came easier, in actual dreary truth, to be good and behave decently, as he did at work and in the flat which was his home. Though he never formulated the idea there is no doubt that he looked forward to full adulthood when he could behave well without the scorn of his friends pouring on him.

So now he squatted on the apple box in the faint drizzle and thought about the implication of tonight's misadventure. He had no illusions about the loyalty of W. Sledge. If indeed he had killed his Kensington old lady, Joe was going to be implicated as deeply as Sledge himself.

He wondered about Queen's Evidence, he'd heard of it but had no idea of the implications other than ... perhaps he could go to the police and tell them about the night's event and he would not be charged with anything.

But somehow that wasn't on the carpet. For some reason or other, he couldn't do it, not out of loyalty to W. Sledge but ... well, he just couldn't do it. Nevertheless, he resolved to bring the subject round somehow, to crime and so on, and get some sort of opinion from his boss, except that Silas would fix him with that awful beady look and say: "What have you been up to, then?"

Having lived so long with someone who was a physical wreck had heightened his own physical sensitivity and he could have screamed with actual pain at the thought of W. Sledge laying in to a frail old lady.

It was April and not actually cold but damp, that strange fog which so often hung over the river whilst a wind whined round the flats, meant that the fog horns mooed rhythmically and this mysterious mooing caused some of the flat-dwellers to demand accommodation elsewhere. "It'll drive me potty!" they would complain, and the kind council would move them to a safe little semi-detached with a tiny plot elsewhere. Others did not notice the sound at all.

To Joe it was something which he had always known, ever since he could remember, the fog and the wind and the fog horns were part of his home life and up on the roof, where he chose to go and sit alone so often, there was the same unearthly quality about the atmosphere that might be sought in the wide open spaces, on some marshy north-country moor or some exposed East Anglian sea-flats with the wild birds' harsh monotonous cry. Though he would never have understood it, up here from the world's slow stain he was, for the moment, secure. Inevitably, after a time, he felt better, refreshed, mindless, he just wanted to stay there; "out of this world," he often called it, at a pinch.

Big Ben gave off one great big deep reverberating note: other bells throughout the City agreed.

And after a long time ... another ... so it was half past one and still he did not want to go in. His father was a very light sleeper and would always shout: "That you, son? G'Night." Never any questions as to where he had been or why he was late in. Never. Dear old Dad.

W. Sledge's ex-home with his parents was on the eighth floor south entrance, and his home with his mistress was on the seventeenth north entrance not facing the river and with a different entrance from those on the river side.The entrances to the individual flats were all on the outside so that every flat had a combined entrance and private balcony on the wall of which they could lean when they wished and look out at the monstrous growth of London below and all around. Not that many of them did, but enthusiastic observers on the south side would claim that at sunset on a clear evening they could see one of Brighton's piers.

The architectural inspiration of an outside entrance to each flat served the useful purpose of causing every tenant to keep their own front entrance clean in the same way that they would brush their own front steps and pathway, and the maintenance men were strict in seeing that this was done. Unfortunately, in spite of the high standard of living, there were those amongst the ninety-two families who still preferred to use the lifts rather than their own lavatories. This was an immense annoyance to Joe's mother, who was proud of her habitation in every other way. "It's folk who come in out of the street," she would declare about once a week, hating the idea that any of her neighbours would so demean themselves and let the community down.

Joe began to feel better, the old familiar mooing, the soft wet wind, the soothing mist were having their effect, his heart slowed down to normal, his brain lay down and slept, he began to feel sleepy. He wanted to fall off the apple box and lie all night where he was.

It looked as though somebody else was doing just that, a few yards away. He rubbed his face, stretched, yawned. It was like Sledge to dash away in the car, not come in and go up to bed in his own flat. He had to dispose immediately of the goods he had stolen and had no doubt told the receiver exactly when he would be arriving. Maybe he was back home and in bed with his lovely mistress by now.

Maybe, Joe thought, he had imagined it all. Maybe he had been half expecting something to go wrong with Sledge's chosen career, he had been too successful for too long.

It was his nerves . . . maybe: he often complained of his nerves, did
Sledge. Joe thought he saw someone asleep across there, in the shelter
of a lift shed too. Slipping he must be, slipping. Getting old. Expecting
trouble all the time, anticipating trouble . . . like his poor Mum did.

He stood up and stretched again. He could do with a toffee or two,
he thought pleasurably of a tin of sweets in his kitchen. He climbed over
a line of pipes, being careful not to touch them because he knew how
dirty they were. He went over to what he had thought was a sleeping
person and it was, indeed, a sleeping person. He leaned closer. A girl,
no less! Coloured? Yes, she had a big black smudge on her cheek. She
was not black, though. She was wrapped in a striped black and white
fun-fur coat and had long, long twiggy kind of legs. A wide black belt
drew in the waist of the coat, making her look like some enormous
damaged wasp in the half-light.

He pushed her with his foot and she sat up instantly, knowing at once
where she was, and possibly who and why. She sat cross-legged, very
self-contained, and said: "Who the hell are you?" And lo! Her voice was
by no means the familiar cockney but something classy like his boss Silas.

Joe looked at her with the interest of a doctor who knew all the
conditions and all the symptoms of those conditions. What was *her*
trouble? Pregnant? An imminent baby? Doped? A junky waiting for the
chemists to open? A north-country or Irish girl come to the metropolis
to take up a career of prostitution? Whatever caused her to settle down
to sleep on the roof of Fiery Beacon was not good or innocent and
that was for sure. He stepped back a little and continued to stare at her
thoughtfully. "Well?" she said defiantly, "I'll bet you've no more right
up here than I have. So you needn't look so cocky."

Cocky! The cheek of it, it was his place, his very own pad, since he
was ten he had come up on the roof for a quiet think, there had never
been anybody to share it with him. Sometimes he had seen workmen
up here and had hidden from them, but this exact spot where he lugged
the apple box, years ago, was private.

"Eff off," he exclaimed automatically.

"You eff off!" she screamed, "disturbing my lovely peace!"

He was aghast. He stepped nearer in order to see her better but she
snatched the corners of the collar of her coat and clutched them round
her like some frightened Victorian miss.

"It's not your bloody roof . . ." she started.

"S . . . sh! You'll wake someone."

"If you don't look out," she hissed, "I'll kick you over; if you fell down there there wouldn't be a piece of you left bigger'n a matchbox!"

"Why, you bloodthirsty little . . ." he couldn't help smiling.

"Get out, get out of my sight," she snarled between clenched teeth and she shook her head violently so that the short hair flew out all round in the pattern of a mop being shaken out of a window.

"Now look," he said reasonably.

"Get out, get out, get out!" She stood up as though preparing to attack him and in her wild and woolly coat she looked bigger than the biggest possible wasp, a wasp more like some crumpled and injured sea bird, crash-landed on the roof of Fiery Beacon on its way up the Thames, screaming with fright and pain.

He hadn't laughed for ages, because young people are not amused. Unless it is nervous laughter or mocking laughter. But something about her made him giggle richly and irrepressibly.

"Oh ho ho!" he laughed, and as an anti-climax he brought out a grubby handkerchief and wiped his eyes, saying at the same time: "You tickle me!" not meaning it literally.

"I *will* tickle you in a minute," she said threateningly. "Do go away."

But he could no more go away than a fly could un-gum itself from a flypaper.

He sat down, leaning on one elbow, he half lay and brought out a toothpick, as a countryman would pick up a piece of straw, and rooted about amongst his teeth, an action denoting constructive thought.

"This is a night and a half!" he observed, thinking out loud, making remarks unconnected one to another. She squatted cross-legged again, her face on a level with his. "There is fairies at the bottom of my garden this bloody night," he declared. "You don't look real," he remarked, "perhaps I've died and you're not real but a spook."

"Nothing is real up here," she said, "how could it be? It's out of this world."

"That's just what I always say: out of this world!"

"One step in the wrong direction and you *are* out of this world."

"Um. In pieces no bigger than a matchbox!" he quoted, smiling at her, but she did not return the smile and looked away hurriedly. "But seriously," he went on, "I've come up here since I was a kid, it is my place, honest."

"Do you live here, then?"

"Yes, down below." He thumped his foot on the asphalt. "My Dad's lying just down below there, waiting for me to come in, shouldn't wonder."

"Why don't you go, then?"

He frowned. "I got somethin' on my mind, see?"

"Haven't we all!" she said sadly.

"Why don't you come down home," he suggested. "My Dad is a cripple, can't move; there's three bedrooms, my Mum's away; you could sleep in her bed, if you like, just for one night," he added in the kind of language Silas used and something like his accent: "our guest!"

She said nothing.

"It's better'n sleeping up here. I tried it once, it was in the summer, too. But cor! It got cold towards morning, I've never known anything so cold, shiverin' I was. Thought I'd catch me death."

No response.

"Look, my Dad won't even know you're there if you keep quiet and don't screech like a seagull."

Silence.

"I could make you a cuppa hot Nescaff, eh? How about it?"

He had evidently touched a soft spot. She stood up, then staggered slightly, holding herself still by placing her hand on the side of the shed.

"Promise I'll sleep alone?"

He nodded, regretful.

"And can I have some cheese and bread?"

He nodded, then seeing how wobbly she was, he put his arm round her and they descended.

Big Ben boomed twice, the city bells sounded too, again confirming the big one's statement.

A guest. So she slept alone, and in the morning he came in carrying a cup of tea, with the contents splashing into the saucer, and put it down on the night table. Keeping her eyes squeezed shut and holding the bedclothes tightly up to her chin she said nothing, pretending to be asleep.

He went across to the door and shut it but staying inside, and sure enough she opened her eyes, though not relaxing her hold on the sheet. He asked no questions, knowing that a bombardment of questions was something one endured from the older generation. But that did not mean there were not very many questions to which he did not want to know the answer, such as, where was her "gear," that is her handbag, etcetera. An adult would have asked who she was, why she had been up to the roof, why she carried nothing, where she came from . . .?

They exchanged, in whispers, semi-serious remarks about the comfort of the bed, the strong sweet tea, and one another. Her coat lay on the floor at the foot of the bed like a large dead dog, the inevitable black polo-necked jersey, the fragmentary skirt, a pink bra and panties lay around, too.

"I think I should warn you," he murmured, "that somewhere between nine and half past a coupla women come in to do for Dad. They've got their own key."

"Do you mean to say he can't move at all?"

"Hardly. But he's all there, mind, so keep your voice down, otherwise he'll wonder. It's fantastic, what he takes in when his body's like, well, as lifeless as that coat there. I'm just taking him a cuppa . . ."

"Do you have to feed him?" she asked, wide-eyed.

"He can move his hands a bit . . ." he demonstrated the pathetic walking of the fingers towards the object the hand required, "he can pick up his drinking cup and get his head down to it; he slops it over but it's better to let him have a go on his own, they've told us. One day he won't be able to move at all and that will be it."

She stared at him thoughtfully. "How awful."

"It's something you get used to; he's marvellous, really; he's happy. They wash him and deal with him and lift him into his chair and wheel him into the living-room and he sits there all day, thinking. He won't have a telly, can you beat it? He has the steam radio, though, and listens to the news and that; he knows more about things in general than most folk, does my Dad."

"So you love him?" she whispered.

"Oh no!" he protested, "not that!" and shuffled his feet about restlessly. "I'm not that soppy, but what I mean to say is: you'd best clear out before these females come, it's eight now so there's no immediate hurry."

Emerging very slightly from the bedclothes she put forth a skinny arm and took a sip of the tea, made a face, then whispered: "I'm looking for a bloke."

She would be. "In this block?"

"Um."

"What's his name?"

"Don't know."

"Young or old?"

"Young."

"Phew ... I reckon you've got a job. There's ninety-odd families in Fiery Beacon; nearly all of them has kids, some of them has grown-up kids who've left home, married, gone away ... others have school kids, and others have babies, toddlers you'll see playing around all day long, up and down the stairs, when it's wet, they're a regular nuisance! You'll never find him, never, not if you don't know his name."

Her lips disappeared, she looked plain for the moment. "I'll find him if it means calling at every flat in the block. I've got to."

Just as I thought, he thought, pregnant. Pathetic. Some folk didn't know how to look after themselves.

"I know what you're thinking," she chuckled. "You look just like a shocked old vicar, it's written all over your face. Oh, grow up! Sorry, I didn't mean to be nasty, you've been so kind. Now, buzz off, I've got to get up and get cracking. If you'd kindly give me a bit of bread and jam or something before I go ... oh, I'm not leaving the district, I might even have to come back this evening, after my day's work combing this block of flats with a small toothcomb."

"Why not take a short cut and ask the police to help?"

"That's a silly idea."

He agreed that it was and an expedient of which he would be the last to avail himself, Queen's Evidence or not, when it came to the crunch. Not that he respected any individual policeman, they were no better than anyone else, it was the great force behind them, the data, the sheer efficient machinery that frightened.

"The police!" she hissed scornfully, and using the expression she had instantly caught from him she invited him to eff off, which he did, feeling that he had not made a success of his visit.

The tea in the pot on the kitchen table had cooled off considerably because he had omitted to use the tea-cosy which his mother always carefully put over the pot. He brought the kettle to the boil again and filled the teapot, then poured out the hot weak tea into his father's drinking cup and carried it in.

One had to walk with care across to the bed; all the ingenuity of well-wishers to make the cripple's life easier had been given a trial, so that the room bore a strong resemblance to something constructed by Emmett. The bed was encased in a metal framework similar to a four-poster which carried any gadget which any amateur inventor had thought up, surrounding the one splendid benefit, a sling on pulleys by which one could raise the inert patient a foot or two above and re-make the bed.

The shell of a man lay, bright-eyed, against his pillows. By means of one of the inventions he had already drawn back the curtains and though the window-sill was not quite low enough to allow him to actually see the river, he could see what kind of morning it was.

So much of him was dead that his eyes seemed abnormally bright sparklers. "Lo, son. Wotcha!"

"Wotcha, Dad!"

"One of them Bo-oing crashed, all on board dead."

"Go on! Where?" Joe looked out of the window, down on to the mist.

"Guatemala."

"I say, I say!" he murmured absently (copying Silas); anything about an old woman battered to death in Kensington, he wondered. But there wouldn't be time; no one would have found her yet. And anyway, they didn't tell you about these acts of violence on BBC radio very much, might make people scared, spread alarm and confusion. "I say, I say!" he picked up an *Evening Standard* which had fallen from the bed-table, glancing at it whilst murmuring, "When do you reckon Mum will be back?"

"Today, maybe. Isn't it fine, Joe, isn't it fine, our Betty with two kids at one go!" The cripple could still smile.

Joe stroked his chin like some elder stroking his beard.

"Or don't you think it a good idea, dragging two more innocents into this vale of tears?" his father quizzed.

"Makes no difference to me," Joe returned sternly, un-equal to light conversation today. "What time's Mum coming?"

"You going to meet her at the air terminus?" his father asked eagerly.

He scowled. "Not bloody likely," he returned. His father was not worried, he knew his Joe. His bark, to coin a phrase, was a lot worse than his bite. He was compelled to put on this parent-hating act, if he did not do so, he could not tolerate living at home, he would have gone off on his own somewhere long ago. So for pride's sake he swore and looked sulky and banged about the place, left his room a great deal more untidy than any pigsty, told them nothing about what he did during the day or night and behaved most of the time like a dissatisfied lodger.

They didn't mind, they not only put up with it, they would have been disturbed had it been otherwise; they loved him.

"But what time's the plane?"

"She's not let me know yet, I reckon she'll telephone. But you're on evening shift this week, Joe boy."

He nodded. "But I'm busy today; haven't time to meet Mum!"

"Okay. Okay. She'll get a taxi. Our Betty'll miss her but I'll be glad to see her back!"

So would Joe ... except that the "guest room," in other words, his mother's own room, could hardly be occupied with its present tenant; there would have to be some explanation, and he was certain that there wasn't going to be. That was the worst thing about one's parents, and others' too, as far as he had heard. They always had to know the why and wherefore of everything. Joe had his pretty well trained by now but there were some things that had to be explained, not many, he knew, but the girl in his mother's room was one. If she had had any gear, had carried a handbag, or a hand-grip of some sort, it might be easier, but she patently did not; furthermore, she was upper class, and that in itself would have to be explained, and couldn't.

So would Joe ... except that he would have to go out soon and buy an evening paper, on the stands by ten-thirty, to see if the thing in the Kensington block of flats had been discovered ... or not. And if not, there would still be the worry. Except that he knew for certain it had happened; W. Sledge had been so near to it for so long; everyone knew him, knew about this fearful streak of violence and yet, with it all, that yellow streak too, that made Sledge sick and vomiting whenever he had really lost his temper or nerve. A frightening friend for anyone to have, but a fascinating one; siphoning off all the fundamental craving for adventure in those more homely than himself.

And besides, look where W. Sledge had got himself, no company director could have done better in the short time ...

Joe sighed heavily: "Yeh, I've a lot to do."

He was sitting at the kitchen table, spreading marmalade on his thick slice of bread when she skipped in lightly and closed the door behind her; she was carrying her fun-fur coat, so she was clearly on her way. He cut her some bread and shoved the butter and marmalade across the littered table.

"I've left the room just as I found it," she whispered.

"So you're off, eh?"

"Um, but I want some paper and a ball-point pen. Have you a notebook to spare?"

"Notebook?"

"Any old kind of notebook would do."

"Mum's got a newish one she hardly ever uses ..." he was fumbling about in a kitchen drawer and finally brought out the red-backed exercise book.

"Will this do?"

"Fine, if I'm going to do some market research. What about a pen?"

"How do you mean—market research?"

"Going from door to door, asking the housewife questions."

"How does that help anybody?"

"Well, by the time I've done this block of flats from top to bottom, or bottom to top might be better, I'll know something about who lives here."

"I can't see how that's going to help you find your boy friend."

"Can't you? Well, I can't help that." She snatched the ball-point pen from him with satisfaction, putting it carefully in the middle of the exercise book. "Suppose it runs out?" she said.

"You'll have to buy another, won't you?"

"What with? Milk bottle tops?"

Heavily, like the ancient "horse leach who hath two daughers crying give! give!" he fumbled in his hip pocket and brought out a pound note. No, a ten shilling note, which he handed across the table.

"Christ! You're a saint! The only saint Bogey!"

He started with surprise that she should know his name but she held up the milkman's chit: "Mrs. Bogey, week ending April 4th" ...

He said: "Call me Joe!"

She started to laugh but stifled it at once. "Joe Bogey! It isn't true."

"It's a Huguenot name," he murmured.

"Huguenot! You're joking!"

He looked contemptuous.

"Very posh!" she whispered. "Joseph Bogey, Esquire, Fiery Beacon, London, SW3. And I see you have a telephone too!"

"Why not? We're priority because of me Dad."

"Priority, whatever next?"

He looked meaningfully at the electric clock.

"Yes, I'm on my way." She pushed the large remaining bit of bread into her mouth and jumped up, mumbling: "I'll be seeing you, then."

Would she? He wondered. Superficially he felt a great indifference as to whether he would or whether he would not be seeing her.

She leaned towards him, she smelled nice somehow, her breath was nice; was she making a pass at him? No, she was leaning forward for him to hear better: "Thank you for this ten bob. It means I can have a meal of some kind."

"Haven't you any money at all, kid?"

She shook her head and her mouth tightened again as at some memory.

"But that won't last!"

"No, I bet it won't!" He was impressed, at least, by her sense of purpose; he felt she meant business, whatever that business was.

"When did you say your Mum was coming back?"

"I didn't say," he grunted.

She said: "Well, I'll be seeing you," and tripped out quietly, shutting the door behind her without a sound.

But like the Cheshire cat, inexplicitly smiling, she was back.

"My name's Frances Smith."

"Can't you think up a better one than that?"

"My Dad's a country gentleman in the Midlands. I thought that would annoy you. He communicates best with horses . . . I said with *horses!*"

"Sh . . . sh!"

"My Mum, not being a horse, left him."

"Ho yeh?"

"She's a bolter, that's what he calls her, which was what probably attracted my Dad to her in the first place. Not all bolters are horses, har har! She's living with what was a terribly good-looking RAF type on a barge in Amsterdam; has been for years, but golly, he's old. As a matter of fact, they're both getting old now ..." She sketched with her finger on her own face, the lines on their faces. "It's loneliness keeps them together more than love." She looked and was dreamily wise, her face falling into sadness momentarily. "They went to Amsterdam in the full flower of their passion, tra la, to escape from their friends; well, they escaped from their friends all right but now they're darned lonely, if you ask me."

"I didn't ask you."

"No, you didn't, that's why I'm telling you. I was ten when she went for the last time. So you see there is plenty of reason for me being a Problem Child."

"Ho, you're one of those!" Joe succeeded in looking sophisticated and drummed his fingers on the table top to show how uninterested he wasn't. "Do you go and see them, then?"

"Not unless she sends me the cash. Sometimes she comes to see me ..."

"Look, I don't believe a word of it."

"All right, don't. I thought I would reward you with the information, as you hadn't asked anything."

He said. "Are you going to start at the top or the bottom—your market research, eh?"

"Right down in the basement, if there is one, I should say. I should get a list of people living here from the maintenance men or man."

"You'll have a job, I'd doubt if they have a list, as you call it."

"Then I'll just have to have a go without one. Farewell, Joe Bogey."

"But when will I be seeing you?"

"Depends."

"Tar-ra, then ..."

CHAPTER III

"Cor!" he said out loud. The cheek of her! She wasn't beautiful, she wasn't even pretty. But she was different; different from other girls in that she had something to say which wasn't dead ordinary; he had never met a girl who ever said anything worth listening to. In fact, girls weren't made for listening to . . . and she was, well, alive, sort of.

In view of the expected return of his mother, he fetched the empty feeding cup from his father's room, tidied up the kitchen and washed up, leaving things as his mother would hope to find them. He threw the bedclothes over his bed, then banged about, opening and shutting drawers.

"What's up, son?" his father called from his bed.

"Lost my pullover."

"Which one?"

It was the black V-necked one with the large white phosphorescent B on the back, which he usually wore under his zip-fastened shower-proof jacket. He went into his father's room, looking around to see if it was lying about. Then he thought he remembered: "I've left it at work."

Outside the door he leaned over the retaining wall and looked down into the rough patch where the cars were parked. He had not left his pullover at work, but something like it, in that he had torn it off because of the car heating, and thrown it in the back of the Jag before setting out as chauffeur with W. Sledge the night before.

The inhabitants of Fiery Beacon were great Jag owners; they were frequent changers-of-cars but one could reckon on half a dozen Jags parked there in the night. At present he could see only two and in the place which W. Sledge occasionally claimed as his own when he didn't put it in the underground park there was no car parked at all; this was not too surprising as he was usually off on his morning's pimping by nine o'clock. The missing pullover, however, would make a good excuse for calling at his flat.

Downstairs, immediately below, was Mr. Owland, a retired waterman who would come up and play chess with his father. So first call was there: "Mum's expected back today, Mr. Owland, but we don't know when, so Dad's got no dates and would be pleased to see you anytime after they've done him."

Then on down the six flights of concrete steps, which he chose rather than the lift because he descended with as much noise and clatter as he could make, to the seventeenth floor back and S. Ledge's private residence.

He admired Amrita, W. Sledge's mistress, because she was so breathtakingly beautiful but that was all. He had been in bed with her once only and had found it as dull and heavy-going as trying to eat his way through a roll of second-rate cotton-wool. Her promise, however, was beyond praise and though he knew it to be all eyewash, his heart gave a small thud of appreciation when she opened the door, after having carefully observed him through the magnifying precautionary peep-hole which had been let into the flat door at her own special eye-height. To put his own eye to the hole W. Sledge himself was obliged to bend his knees, being nearly two feet taller than Amrita.

Her sari was a miracle of misty blue with, below, the tight short bodice sleeve covering the shoulder and the top of one brown arm with gold metallic material. Though she may have carried out the usual woman's tasks with broom, vacuum and soap flakes, she never showed the slightest sign of it. Not for her the slatternly appearance first thing in the morning. The wind caught her sari and blew it against her with ravishing effect and she smelled fabulously Eastern.

"Sledgey at home?"

She shook her head.

"Mind if I come in a minute?"

She opened the door wide and he entered.

The flat was an essay in interior decorations as far as Joe knew but was in fact a conglomeration of elaborate Indian-cum-European-isms and the chairs were only just chairs, one tiny distance from actual cushions on the floor.

"I left my pullover in his car last night. Black with my initial on the back, all lit-up white, seen it?"

She shook her head.

"Lost your voice, have you?"

She laughed a little, then her face went serious, worried even.

"What's up, Amrita love?" Not for the first time Joe's mind was on the mystery of that tight golden sleeve under the sari: was it part of a vest, or what? how far did it extend? Amrita was not one clumsily to let you watch her undress; she would retire gracefully and call to you when you were allowed to enter her room, to find her lying naked on the bed. But seriously, was it a whole garment or only one quarter of a garment? He wasn't even listening for her answer when she surprised him by saying something in her dove-like voice.

"He is not well . . ."

Joe dragged his mind back from his immediate thoughts.

"I didn't think he was. What's wrong?"

"He's been sick, you know how he is. He will never tell me but I know, he's been in some kind of trouble. If you were with him last night you must know."

"Not me."

She looked sad, hanging her head and murmuring, "You will not tell *me*, of course."

"Where is he now?"

"He went out early, long before daylight, didn't come to bed at all; he has gone to have something done to the car, I think, because I think I heard him telephoning the night watchman at the garage where he sometimes goes, where he bought the Jag, early, and asked if it was all right to bring it."

"Yes," Joe agreed; "I didn't think he was well. He was very sick in the car last night."

"No fighting?"

Joe shook his head. "Not that I know of."

"He didn't sleep all night; I promise you . . . he didn't come to bed; he sat in here and sometimes he got up and went to the bathroom and was sick."

"If he's been sick all that often likely it's a tummy upset, food poisoning, eh?"

"I have given him much milk, he lives on his nerves that boy; one day he will go mad perhaps and kill me."

She had said that before, it was of no interest. Sadly she knew that her remark would produce no reaction, she often complained that one day she would leave Sledge but that did not ring a bell with anyone either; always they looked but did not listen. Joe simply went: "Um!"

"I have lived more than eighteen months with him and he tells me nothing, ever, for a year and a half."

Joe thoroughly sympathised with his friend there; a beautiful apathetic bird was just the job, exactly what an up and coming young man required, asked no questions and always said yes, in fact yes was the only significant word she could be guaranteed to utter.

"When he gets in one of his tempers, he beats me," she said, head down but looking up at him through her fringe of lashes.

"You need it, I daresay," Joe returned darkly, shocked slightly but not going to show it. He sensed a distinct loosening in the threads that held the Amrita—W. Sledge relationship together. One of these days old Sledgey was going to come home and find the bird had flown. He wondered whether he should warn him or whether it would precipitate one of Sledge's frightening rages. But he added kindly: "Getting sick of him, are you?" Phrasing his question in the manner of anyone of his set, aware that the question they were asking was of a personal and delicate nature. It sounded much better than a plain, straightforward, blunt question: Are you getting sick of him? It was gentler and felt less like a question.

Anyway, she didn't answer but simply shrugged.

"Well, tell him I called." He waited for some response, there was none. "Well, tar-ra, then."

He enjoyed clattering down the concrete steps to the eighth floor. It would have been a super experience if the staircase had been made spirally, as well it might, but no doubt the builders knew all about the fun you could have, whizzing round and round a spiral staircase until you couldn't stand up. They had meanly constructed the staircase round a narrow well beside the lift shaft and service area, with small landings every dozen steps and no light beyond the occasional bracket, so that lingering on the staircase was not attractive.

W. Sledge's father was a sour bus-driver, sour because most of his day was spent breathing in diesel fuel fumes, feeling ill and adding to the carcinogens in his lungs by chain smoking; he had no interests, he felt too rotten to go out to his favourite pub except on Sunday mornings. When he came home at night he flung himself into a comfortable chair in front of the television and his wife served him with tele-snacks. There was no conversation between the couple because there was nothing to talk about except how awful he felt and there was no point in talking about it because it was all too obvious.

His wife was a sharp-tongued woman with blazing red hair; in her earlier life she had been a post office clerk but had been sacked for pilfering. She hated being an office Mrs. Mop getting up every morning at four o'clock and working till 8.30, but she was well paid though she spent a large proportion of her earnings on Bingo, to which she went twice a week, never winning anything worth having but always hopeful.

Mrs. Sledge's mouth was full, she was having breakfast when Joe called. Having opened the door to him she immediately sat down at the kitchen table and went on having it. He stared at her tea-cosy, which was really obscene, the stuffing bursting out, it was black with grease, an object for a coal hole rather than a table. With part of his mind Joe thought complacently about the okay tea-cosy at home in mock patchwork quilting, that he had omitted to use that morning.

"Come to tell me our Winston has been up to something?" Mrs. Sledge guessed. "He didn't come home this weekend, he didn't. We haven't seen him for ten days. Oh that boy! One of these days there'll be a dick at the door and I'll drop dead, sure as I'm sitting here I will."

"I just wondered . . ."

"Yes, what?"

"We were out together last night and I left my pullover in his car; I just wondered . . . He was sick, Mrs. Sledge, in the car."

"Well, that's a bad sign, for a start!"

"That's what I thought, I thought . . ."

"Sick, was he? Highly strung, that brain doctor I took him to said. It's his nerves, takes after me. Feels things!" she explained. "Oh, he was a naughty boy, it was only luck kept him from one of these approved schools. I did my best; he went on and on and on, doing the same thing no matter how often I told him not to. And when I smacked him, no I had to thrash him with a slipper, he was sick."

Joe had heard all this before, he knew he would have at least to appear to be listening but he was worried to the point of being sick himself; he knew W. Sledge as well as his mother knew him, if not better.

" . . . So don't ever punish him, never lay a finger on him in anger, those was the doctor's very words, his very words. I reckon I'm glad

I don't have any more kids, they're more trouble than they're worth, really they are!"

"But the point is ..."

"And the cheek of it, living up there in Colindale and won't even give us the address. Suppose one of us really was to drop dead? His Dad's none too well. We couldn't even let him know if anything happened, we'd be dead and buried by the time he turned up 'ome. He 'likes his freedom' he says. Cor! I'd give him freedom if I had my way!" She was lashing herself into a state. Joe wished he had not come but he had felt that maybe, perhaps W. Sledge had decided to come home last night for a little bit of sympathetic mother-love, for a change.

He tried to go but she detained him, saying everything she had said and much more in the same vein, over again. If he had not disliked her, he might have been sorry for her, she had no chance of a good talk in her home life, unless she talked to herself.

Finally he extricated himself and went to look in the north-side car park to see if the Jag had returned. It had not. He leaned against the railings and watched the river, half hoping that the Jag would turn up but knowing that if W. Sledge was having a successful morning there would be customers and his sensitivities would forbid his return until evening.

TREBLE CHANCE WIN FOR BLIND MAN

the first edition of the evening paper mildly announced and Joe went to a coffee-bar in Soho where he met some friends and stayed until late afternoon, during which the evening papers had received news worth shouting about:

GENERAL'S WIDOW FOUND STRANGLED

not a first-class selling line such as those on the posters which the newsmen kept to intrigue the shoppers up in the West End for a "shopping spree," such as SON FOR SOPHIA LOREN or ROYAL DIVORCE HITCH.

But one citizen, however, was deeply affected by the headline; though he had been expecting it, when it finally came he was hit amidships, a crashing blow.

With poisoning, drowning, shooting, pushing out of the window and even hanging, "foul play" could often be discounted and suicide suspected instead. But with strangling there was no let out, nobody ever strangled themselves successfully.

He bought a paper, his fingers shaking so much that he could scarcely hold it still enough to read it: " ... the widow of General Sir Edward Bellhanger of Tripoli fame ... an interrupted burglary ... son supplied a list of missing silver objects to the police ..." The sort of thing that appeared only too often, he almost knew it by heart.

He crushed the paper up angrily and threw it down. It had come to this, he ought to have known that it would. W. Sledge had been altogether too successful, too confident, too boastful, too contemptuous of others; he had become careless, thought himself immune from ordinary mishaps; there was nothing he couldn't do in his own opinion. That inherent violence of his. . .

He was a spoiled boy, Joe considered, someone who had had everything he had wanted always and then, when he was frustrated, suddenly saw that he would be deprived of this snuff-box haul he had planned so cheerfully and confidently, he had to brush aside, in fact, exterminate, that which was standing in the way of immediate success.

It was the spoilt boys, Joe thought bitterly, who did the murdering; the deprived ones, like himself, were too used to being deprived to do anything other than stick the frustrations; he had heard these sober and serious discussions about the young delinquents on the radio and they made him blow rude raspberries.

He'd known all these things all along but nonetheless, they had not caused him to drop his friendship with W. Sledge; it was because of them, rather than in spite of them, that he enjoyed his friendship, or had done so to date; he had been privileged to know W. Sledge, in fact, had been proud of the fact that W. Sledge confided in him and treated him as a friend and servitor.

So now, Joe Bogey was about to smash up this friendship for ever; he would do the only sensible thing, which was to take himself off immediately to Chelsea Police Station and tell them the whole story. It was the only sensible thing to do, he kept repeating to himself: to tell a policeman.

He was standing in Piccadilly Underground, sheltering from the drizzle, crowds passing, no one looking at him or, indeed, at anyone else. Unobservant, intent upon their own business, hundreds and hundreds of people! Nobody of the passing thousands knew who he was; he had no distinguishing marks; Joe Bogey and his ridiculous surname could come to an end from now on. Simply vanish.

But he could not do it for a very elementary reason; though under torture he would never have admitted it, he loved his family; he simply could not inflict the misery upon them that he would by disappearing.

And it was only when he had travelled two miles and stood within a few yards of Chelsea Police Station he decided not to go in and tell his story for the same, and what seemed to him utterly nauseating, very simple reason.

And since simplicity seemed to be the keynote of today's thinking, he decided to trust his luck which, so far, had not failed him. W. Sledge was a lucky type too; in fact, Sledgey's luck up to now had been fantastic, almost a legend in their set; maybe this would hold and the murder of the General's old lady would go into the dossier amongst the many unsolved crimes. By this time next week . . . over and forgotten, even by the police themselves, since there would be a lot to fill their minds between now and this time next week; several more murders and a bloodless revolution in Trafalgar Square on Sunday afternoon, to say the least.

It would be utterly selfish of him, Joe decided, to tell the police all he knew about last night's robbery and cause his family endless anguish, simply in order to clear himself (or perhaps indict himself, who knew?).

So turning his back on the Police Station and walking rapidly away he swore aloud; using words which somehow winged back to him from the days when he and his sister were forced by their mother to go to Sunday school: "I swear that I shall never help W. Sledge again in the name of the Father, the Son and the Holy Ghost and that means for ever, so help me God, Amen." He licked his fingers and crossed his heart.

Silas was out when he arrived at work. Mrs. James Trelawny was elegantly pushing the mop over the floor of the bar. "Well, my dear Joe," she said kindly, "how is everything with you?"

Joe always felt she was making fun of him but she wasn't a bad old stick, giving him a good tip come Christmas; part of her payment being a pizza to herself before she left work, Joe would take special trouble over this "solo" as he called it, giving her mushroom instead of aubergine, which she did not like because she always used to pick out the bits.

But this was something between them that she had the tact never to mention; nothing would have annoyed Joe more than to be thought considerate. Whilst he was making her pizza, inevitably she picked up the evening paper and glanced at the headlines, clicking her tongue disapprovingly at what she read.

"Oh dear, oh dear, oh dear!" she sighed as Joe put down the food in front of her, and the knife and fork daintily wrapped in their napkin. "Being poor has its advantages; no burglar's likely to break in on me for my silver gadgets because I haven't got any ... that's one comfort."

He made a point of not responding to Mrs. James Trelawny's monologues; wearing his habitual expression of disgust and contempt he withdrew behind the counter and concentrated on making his lines of vegetable on the uncooked pastry. He had washed his hands, pulled on his horizontal-striped apron, tied the cotton square sweat rag round his neck, put on his chef's hat as though everything were as usual.

But how much further away he was from this time last evening, when the prospect of having his own bar seemed almost within his reach. Last time he had made these same movements, arranging his pieces with such care, how happy, free and adventurous the prospect had seemed, and now ... how black and fearful the future: he was a wanted criminal, or at least the paid assistant of a wanted criminal. How was it that he had never thought it might happen?

But he had, that was it, he had.

What would now happen to his brave fellow-clubmen of The Wotchas, meeting usually on Wednesdays in the cafe in the wrong end of Chelsea? Some of them had graduated from watchers to performers themselves and Joe had been considered one of the slow ones, poor chap, still living with his family; he knew they thought him a softy. How were they feeling now? Some of them smoked marihuana; one or two of them had gone the way of harder stuff and had been dropped because they had become sloppy and untrustworthy. Joe himself had never smoked pot because, quite simply, it gave him a headache and he did not experience the heightened enjoyment of the moment of which others boasted.

Mrs. Trelawny organised the washers-up and kept a keen eye on the customers so that none of them escaped without paying, until Silas arrived half-way through the evening, having evidently been to a party because he was dressed in his excellent dark mauve velvet jacket and bow tie. The bar was full, the air redolent with a delicious appetising smell and the owner mooched about, tall and droopy, having a word here and there with those who were feeling pleasant amongst his motley customers.

Joe worked hard, still taking some pleasure in arranging each tray of pastry differently so that there were no two patterns of vegetables alike. The evening wore on; what if W. Sledge appeared again like last night? Since he had sworn never again to have anything to do with him it was going to be awkward.

Besides . . . he would owe Joe money for last night's assignation, his percentage on the night's takings, if there had indeed been robbery, as the paper had said there had. One thing of which Joe was sure was that if there had been a robbery W. Sledge would have disposed of the loot within the hour, or less. That was one of the things which made him seem reliable; he inspired the confidence of his selection of receivers and they never failed him; the day after he had done a job he would come up with the money for his Wotchas without fail. So what was he going to do if he came? "Eff off, and take your (literally) bloody money with you"?

Pulling the last sizzling tray of the evening out of the oven Joe stood above it, hands on his hips, and surveyed the eaters, thinning out now, towards midnight.

At a nod from Silas he came out from behind the counter with a plate of the pizza which he put on the table by the door in front of the boss. He took a plateful himself and sat down at the table nearest to the counter; picking up a fork he started his own supper; he got up and helped himself to a Pepsi-Cola and sat down again.

His mind was so far away and his memory suffering from shock trauma that he did not at once recognise the girl when she came in; most girls who came into the pizza bar had boys with them, they nearly all wore their hair down to their shoulders and longer and looked deathly ill; this girl was unlike the others in that her hair was short, like a boy's, and she looked healthy. That striped fur coat too!

From somewhere, way, way back in his dim past, he remembered her and swore. It was the familiar exercise book she was carrying which he vaguely recognised. He now had worries enough without this waif and stray.

She came over to him at once, leaning across the table and hissing
dramatically: "Oh Joe, for God's sake give me something to eat; I've been
waiting for you for hours, absolutely hours."

"How did you know where I was?" he asked sulkily.

"I went to your flat. I had to, Joe; I tell you I'm starving."

An intercom telephone had been fixed in the Bogeys' flat in such a
way that when the bell was pressed at the front door his father was just
able to pick up the receiver and press the button to open the front door,
if he so wished, when he heard the caller's business.

Reluctantly Joe got up and filled yet another plate with food;
bringing it to her, and putting it down smartly in front of her, he sat
down scowling.

"I rang the bell and your father answered, I said I was a girl friend
of yours . . . she looked defiantly across the small table at him. "He said
to come in, wanted to have a look at me I suppose, but I said I hadn't
time and where did you work? So he asked my name and I told him; he
sounded as though he was lonely."

"So Mum's not back?"

"I've had nothing to eat all day, only cups of tea offered me. I didn't
spend any of the ten bob you gave me, only getting here."

She was enjoying her food, simply shovelling it down; soon she was
ready for another. Silas was eyeing them across the room, it was nearly
closing time; Joe got up and brought her another pizza.

"Did you make these?"

"Um!"

"Lovely!"

"Look," Joe said patiently, "last night's rooftop meeting was all right,
nothing's quite real up there, it was like a dream; but it can't go on." He
gesticulated feebly before her aghast expression, "I mean I haven't time, I
simply haven't time for . . . for this responsibility. Haven't you any money
. . . or a friend in London, or something?"

"No, I haven't, only the ten bob you gave me, can't you see I haven't?
That's the whole point!" There were only two customers left in the
bar and Silas was lighting his last Balkan Sobranie of the evening. "I'm
derelict, don't you realise? I mean destitute . . ." Predictably she started
to cry. "I've been robbed by that beastly red-haired bloke in your block
of flats, whatever his name is . . ."

"How do you know him?"

"I don't know him," she practically screamed querulously. "I've come to London to get a job because I'm not staying at home one more day, not one more hour, in fact! So, of course, I get picked up instantly, would you believe it? But he's not bad looking, or so I thought, and he's full of beans . . ."

She sobbed openly now, in the absence of a handkerchief she wiped her eyes on the tablecloth and her nose on the back of her hand. "I was on my way to look for a room in Chelsea I saw advertised in the newspaper shop window, and I thought I'd have a cup of coffee first at one of those dark, fascinating coffee bars in King's Road. And well he . . . you know, I don't have to tell you, surely. He was kind and helpful, said he could put me in the way of getting a job in a clothes' shop a few streets away. So . . . well, I went with him. It was a fairly kinky place called 'I Was Napoleon's Mistress,' can't say I liked it much but they said I could start next week. Then he said as that was done and it was a nice day, why not come for a run in the car? He'd got a Jag parked in an underground car park not far away, and off we went, down to Maidenhead along the M4. Phew! He went so fast I screamed. He teased me, going faster and faster, I was frightened out of my wits."

She stopped to pile some of the second pizza into her mouth.

"And then?"

"It was nice down by the river. We walked about a bit and I—that is—and he said it was too cold to make love, and besides, he said, he was busy in the evening. So I started wondering where I was actually going to spend the night; I've lots of friends who share flats with other girls in London but I couldn't trust one of them not to tell my father where I was. Most of them come home for the weekends and they all think my father's a jolly good sort, everyone does."

She became thoughtful for a moment.

"And so?"

"So he dropped me out of the car, that's what. When we were nearly back where we'd started, he opened the door and I got out and when I turned to get my handbag and zipper-case with my things in it he slammed the door in my face and zizzed off. I screamed to a chap in a car behind and he stopped and I told him to follow that Jag, I'd been robbed, and he tried, he really did his best but he didn't know his geography like him, we lost him. Then, of course, I had to have a drink in a pub with this chap who'd been so kind, whose advice to me was to return home quick ... I ask you! He had to go back home to his wife and all I had left to do was to wave good-bye."

Her face was blotchy with dried tears. "Then I had a brainwave, I thought of that shop; it wasn't far away, straight on down that long, long street up a side turning, past the pub called World's End, and it feels like it, too. When I got there ... guess what? It was long past closing time but I saw a dim light down in the basement and there some of them were, smoking pot. I went in and told them the red-haired bloke who'd introduced me had gone off with all the possessions I had in the world and they laughed their heads off. However, one of them who wasn't so, what, high? ... he said he was called Sledge and he lived in a tower block not far from Battersea Bridge, couldn't miss it, he said, and then offered me a marihuana cigarette. I've had them and I knew it wasn't the time for it, I have to keep my head *now*, so I left."

"You told me you didn't know his name," Joe accused.

"I know I did, I thought the chap was making up the name or something because when I called on Mrs. Sledge she slammed the door in my face!"

Her tears had dried rapidly, she simply sat back, replete and sniffing, regarding him expectantly as though awaiting his suggestions for the next move.

"They didn't know the *number* of his flat, otherwise I wouldn't have been up on the roof. All those flats! On my market research rounds I asked lots of people which flat a tall young chap with lots of red hair lived in, nobody could tell me. So I'm absolutely sunk, destitute and on your hands, and that's that!"

"But why on *my* hands?"

"Because you're nice," she said decisively. "It was silly of him (a) not to tell me his name, and (b) to take me to that ghastly shop '*I Was Napoleon's Mistress*', where there were friends of his there who knew him. Or perhaps, thinking it over, greed outweighed his common sense: perhaps he can't help stealing or bag snatching and did it without thinking. But then we both lost our common sense, I ought never to have told him I'd run away from home; he'd guess my handbag was packed with boodle ..."

"With what?" he asked absently. But he was sick at heart, Sledge's action was out of character, as was his further action a few hours later of strangling the old lady. It wasn't *like* him; he was seriously slipping, like going suddenly off his nut.

"Cash; dibs; lolly; nearly two hundred pounds, in fact, two hundred minus my train fare, everything I had in the bank; gifts and saved-up allowance. So, you see, I've got to get it back, got to. I can't go to the blooming police because, because I'm a *minor* minor, what my father calls a mere school-kid. He'll have alerted the whole police force in England, my father will, he'll be having all the ports watched, the airports ... the lot; he's Lord Lieutenant of our county, by the way, and the most charming man anyone has ever met too, so people say, but he's not *my* choice. He has strong stiff upstanding white hair and a round rosy face and big, wide almost continuous smile with all his own teeth and that's the lot. He's the sort of thing a computer would knock up in its spare time if you instructed it to produce: one perfect English gentleman, please. He's a ... a façade, a cardboard ... no, worse, he's a plastic person; I can see right through him and out on the other side. I can absolutely understand why my mother left him and why she'd much rather live on a barge with any old soak than to have to put up with him and his eternal, jolly-good-fellow laughter. He won't divorce her, of course; he could, if he only would, for desertion, but he never will. So everybody says my mother must be mad, how could she leave such a marvellous chap! Huh, huh!"

"So did you tell Sledge all this?"

"Of course I didn't. I did tell him I'd left home, though, *and* for ever, but I didn't tell him about my father and mother being separated *nor* did I tell him why I left home. But if you're really going to help me and go on being kind, I may tell you. It'll wring your heart."

His heart was too sick to be wrung as well, he hardly cared any more.

It was now about two minutes to midnight and Silas was keeping very quiet, probably listening to everything, but it was too late to bother about that now. He was holding *The Times* up in front of him and the smoke from yet another cigarette was rising above it.

"Well, tell me now, quick, I've got to pack up, it's closing time."

"Don't believe slave-selling is over! There was a take-over bid for me, for *me*! One of these business tycoons came to live near, he uses his

Jacobean house as a factory, making cheap flashy shirts and selling them by post; he actually had a deal to buy me off my father's hands."

Joe said: "I was thinking something like that myself, only yesterday, about slavery."

But she wanted to tell her story: "He actually did! Well, I'd liked him to start with; it was fun to be seen about in such marvellous cars with such an evil-looking type . . . but marry him! The very thought makes me heave but heave . . . he wears a *wig*!" she screamed.

Silas cleared his throat; it was a sign for Joe to spring up and make all the late-night movements, which he did whilst the girl sat with her hands deep in her coat pockets, her legs stretched out in front of her, brooding darkly.

Silas walked round her, or mooched thoughtfully about her; she looked up and said she hoped she was not in the way. Joe came out from behind the bar now without his uniform and wearing his waterproof zipped jacket. He took out the relevant amount of money he owed for his girl-friend's supper and handed it to Silas, who already had his hand stretched out for it.

"Thanks," Joe said, looking at his boss.

"What are you going to do with her?" Silas asked.

"I'll take care of her," Joe said, still looking soberly at Silas. He was affronted by the huge wink that Silas gave him, and hustled his girl-friend out in front of him.

CHAPTER IV

They sat stiffly, not touching one another in the taxi, but presently out came her warm gloveless hand and sought his own hand. He folded his fingers round it but said disapprovingly: "Now look! You're a sly one, I know, you've got a hell of a lot to say but it's difficult to know what's true and what isn't. I think, when you're talking, I think: she's inventing all this, I'm sure!"

"Well, I don't blame you," she sighed, "but truth is stranger than fiction (as they say); I've had to keep things bottled up for a long time; the groom at home knows the lot, not because I've told him, but because he's seen it all happen ..."

"Oh, is he a boy-friend?"

"Certainly not; he's got a perfectly good wife, thanks. Only he's sorry for me, I know. I've heard him say it, things like 'Poor kid, what's going to happen to her?' And once I heard him say someone ought to knock his bloody block off, meaning my father. There's just one or two, people who work for him mostly, know what he's really like. Things like my father'll tell his friends: 'I've given my groom his cottage for my lifetime!' he'll say boasting, it sounds fine if you don't start thinking; but what does it mean? Absolutely damn' all, as I heard the groom telling someone. And I overheard Dad talking to a friend one evening: 'I hope I'm not going to lose my darling baby' (that's me!) 'to a man old enough to be her father ... but there it is, she's devoted to him!' "

He couldn't see her face properly but he noted the way her head hung on her long thin neck which appeared, perhaps, abnormally long owing to the shortness of her hair. The taxi lurched round Trafalgar Square with the lights green and she rolled against him; he put an arm round her.

"But ..." he thought carefully, "you don't tell the truth always, do you?"

No answer.

"You tell just what's useful and what isn't?"

"Can't you distinguish between truth and a white lie for convenience?"
"No, I can*not*."
"Well, give me an example of me lying."
"When I first met you I asked you the name of the chap, the bloke
you called him, you were looking for and you *said you didn't know,* that
was a lie for one."
"I had to, of course, silly, he might have been a friend of yours."
"As it happens he is ... was, I mean."
"Oh, so that's his real name? When he asked me my name and I said
Frances Smith, he didn't believe it any more than you did. He made me
swear it and I said only if he told me his name, which he did. I knew it
wasn't right," she said bitterly.
"But it is, he's called Winston Sledge, but he'll never let on to the
Winston because his Mum and Dad called him after some funny old
politician, died a bit ago, Prime Minister or some lark."
"Well, it can't be his real name because ... because one of the caretakers
showed me the names of everybody in the flats and there's one couple
called Sledge and I called on them; as I told you; there was a very bad-
tempered old woman opened the door, masses of red hair and a cross
face, she had, said she didn't know any young chap called Sledge; said
they hadn't any children and never wanted any either ... and slammed
the door shut, as I told you ..."
Battersea Bridge rose in front of them, majestic, belonging to a
different world and retaining its eccentricities with pride. Joe tapped
on the driver's window, they descended and as the taxi moved off they
moved automatically and together on to the bridge, staring along the
river at the reflected light in the translucent, sliding water below.
"It's a mistake not to have told me before, since you're telling me
now," Joe remarked, "you've got yourself into a heck of a mess."
"Yes, I agree. But I must say, there's nothing like a spot of 'market
research' if you really want to get inside people's dwellings. You stand
on the doorstep, pen poised, and 'oozing charm from every pore,'
you indicate that your firm have only one wish in mind and that is to
know what your Mrs. So-and-So does about whatever you decide on;
I decided on breakfast food, I made up the brand name, ARBISCO, it's
a town in North Sweden, I went with friends not long ago, to see the
Midnight Sun. Half way through I thought cosmetics might have got

me going quicker, on the personal side, but then, I wasn't really going round to get their private life history. ARBISCO did very nicely; they opened up with their household problems. It was fun but the worry of finding Sledge spoiled it for me, actually," she complained wistfully. "It took ages, one or two of them couldn't stop talking; it's taken me all day to do about twenty flats. But it's strange what an isolated world you all live in, in Fiery Beacon—nobody I asked had ever heard of Winston Sledge!"

"They're going to!" Joe shuddered. For a time his mind had been taken off his own troubles.

"What?"

"They're going to hear the name Sledge before long."

"Come on, tell me . . ."

That he would certainly not do. Instead he said: "No! But you've got to tell me your proper name."

"How am I to know you're not going straight to the police?"

She had a point there, he would not have done what he asked if he had been she. He was not insulted or annoyed, as he might have been, he simply accepted it sadly.

After a time she felt for his hand again, pressing it and saying: "Well, it honestly is Frances Smith, you can call me Fanny if you like; my father's is a hyphened name."

"What's that?"

"You know . . . something-or-other-Smith, with a hyphen, distinguishes him from the run-of-the-mill, as he'd call it, Smiths."

"I get you."

"But I've decided to drop the something-or-other, there's no law against dropping it, is there?"

He wouldn't know. "Well, tell me just one more thing and I'll never ask another question."

"What is it?"

"Promise you'll tell the truth?"

She thought for a long time, minutes, so that he thought she was going to ignore it. Finally she promised elaborately, as he had done himself earlier, crossing her heart in the old school-girlish way, with licked fingers and a request to God to strike her dead should she tell a lie.

He was so annoyed that he let go of her hand. "It's not that I care all that much about the truth, it's that I don't know where I am with you if you make up facts about yourself."

"Oh, *go on,* I've promised I'll answer truthfully."

He took a little winning round before he came out with it: "You said, when you and Sledge were on the tow-path at Maidenhead, you said *he* said it was too cold ... if he hadn't like ... said that, I mean ... would you of?"

She frowned, trying to understand the question: "You mean ... when he said it was too cold to make love?"

"Um. Would you of?"

"No I wouldn't, I'd have kicked and screamed and fought like mad, I'd have knocked him silly ... with my knee, I'd have rolled into the river and drowned, rather than."

"Oh," he returned inadequately.

"You don't believe me, I suppose?"

"Well, it's very unusual, I mean."

"I won't do it till I get married."

"Why not, everyone does."

"Not *everyone*." She paused and said: "Because I want to have a happy marriage and if I've done all that lot before ... well, it might, it just might, spoil things later on, see?"

He did believe her; he was struck dumb with amazement; he took her hand again and they walked over the bridge.

CHAPTER V

Motherhood had only gradually gone bad on Mrs. Sledge. After the post office pilfering episode she had lowered her sights about the hypothetical man she intended to marry. The actual pilfering had been an effort to pull herself up from the poverty into which she was born, to better herself regarding clothes, hair-dos, manicures and the circle of acquaintances amongst whom she moved.

Having failed, at the age of thirty-five, to find a white-collared husband she decided it was time to settle, if she must, for someone in a lower social scale. She met Sledge one Sunday evening in a public house in the farthest reaches of Chelsea. He was attracted, like a moth to the flame, by her gorgeous red hair, and within four weeks had married her. There being something obscure but immensely interesting about Mrs. Sledge's ovaries (there were either too few or too many), the birth of her perfect boy-child was considered, at the Chelsea Hospital for Women, little short of a miracle; the birth was written up in a gynaecological journal and a record kept in a Book of the Hours.

He was indeed a perfect baby, turning into a delightful-looking toddler. Adults could not keep their hands off him; strong men, with shouts of pleasure, would snatch him up and throw him in the air, catching him again to swing him from side to side, as though he were some kind of cocktail. When left in his parked pram outside the Co-op, old ladies would be so entranced by his looks that they would buy him iced lollies for which they would be rewarded by an angelic smile. As soon as he had finished one there would be someone eager to buy him another so that they too might be rewarded by that smile.

His mother would hurry out saying: "He'd better not have any more, thanks, he'll be sick ..."

Sick? It didn't matter how many iced lollies he had, he was not sick; what did make him sick was not having another.

Since time passes very slowly to a child, this happy period seemed to last a very long time indeed. But as he grew up, it all passed; unaccountably to himself, he was no longer the golden boy, there was no longer any delighted response to his appearance. When his milk teeth fell out in front he looked, rather repulsive; adults would address him in quite a different manner. When he sprouted two big yellow teeth, the ones he was to have for life, they looked quite out of proportion to the rest of his face. When he fell and broke one of them in half on the bottom step of the concrete stairs at Fiery Beacon, his mother shook him: "I'll have to put up with you being an ugly little monster and that's all! No dentist can fix on half a tooth!" And because he was upset he found the cat and tortured it; somehow it made him feel better. He did this in secret for a long time but when his mother found him at it she flew into a very noisy temper and slapped him on the side of the head.

After that the cat disappeared.

He threw it over the balcony rail, outside their front door, whilst his mother was in the lavatory. His mother moaned around for several days, complaining that the cat had left home and she couldn't blame it. Nothing was ever said about the broken little ginger body found eight stories below in the forecourt and thrown into the incinerator by one of the caretakers.

Some time later, when they were both twelve, he told Joe Bogey, as they were sitting together on the low wall at the edge of the playground beside the tower block. Unaccountably, Joe wouldn't believe it, thought he was boasting. "You didn't, you didn't, you didn't!" he shouted.

"All right, I didn't!" young Sledge said soothingly, squatting down and writing "F . . ." in the dust. One day he would show him!

It became important to impress people, since they no longer fell about with cries of delight at the sight of him. He found there were a number of ways in which he could at least impress himself. He would go off alone to the street markets on Saturday and Sunday mornings and practise a technique which, in time, he developed to an art, that of stealing with his head, as it were, turned the other way. He would choose some small article at the very edge of the stall, spending some time over the choice; he would stay in the vicinity so that he became part of the scene and in no way remarkable, then he would "accidentally" knock the article off the table and, at the exact moment when the stall-owner's head was engaged in serving someone, he would crouch down and without looking at the article, would feel for it with one hand and get it into his pocket, whilst staying in that position for perhaps as long as a minute after the act of pilfering; nobody is surprised at a boy's unusual movements such as squatting thoughtfully almost under a stall in a market on Saturday mornings. Young Winston did not know the word subtle; in time he prided himself on being "crafty."

Though his babyhood had been a long, long time, the period between then to puberty passed quickly. The problem of this unruly thing in his trousers was easily solved with the help of two or three grubby little girls in his class at school, on old bombed sites or vacant lots near the World's End or somewhere far enough away from their own neighbourhood, at the weekends.

Whereas at fourteen he had looked four years older than he was, a large ungainly youth whose features had gone ahead of him becoming sharp and pointed, as it were, at eighteen he looked twenty-five, smaller and neater as to body but still with the wild red hair.

"Well, Winston?" his exhausted schoolmaster asked him on his last day at school: "What are you going to be?"

"Me, sir?" It paid to be polite to authority, however much you might despise it. "I'm going for a night-watch-man." Not for him the "tiny breakfast, trolley-bus and windy street."

The schoolmaster laughed: "Ambitious, what?" and young Winston felt his guts wrung by bitter anger; he hated being laughed at, even when it was meant kindly.

Certain concessions, however, had to be made to the demon work, such as the carrying of a few bricks daily for some weeks; making tea in the portable huts for building teams; lowering the back of brick-loaded lorries, sometimes automatically and at other times actually jumping down and unhitching the back so that gravel could be shovelled out. He enjoyed working the concrete mixer, too. He became adept at the art of standing about near groups of workers, or amongst them, so that he gave the appearance of being at work but doing nothing more useful than a cow chewing its cud, less in fact, because he was neither feeding himself nor making milk. He joined a firm of subcontractors who employed men whom they sent round to various sites; a few days here, a week or so there; he could stay away from work whenever he felt like it, absenteeism becoming his favourite pastime.

And there were the final achievements of joining a union and later pouring sweet reason over the heads of the various clerks with whom he had to deal at the Employment Exchange. He spent so much charm on this that he was drained of it when it came to dealing with the old folks at home. He simply couldn't be bothered with them, so interfering, so possessive; they irritated him. Until such time as he chucked them completely they got badly on his nerves and frayed the edges of his temper; his mother particularly, she would not "leave well alone" and let him "get on with it."

In the meantime he opened a banking account because he could not trust that old harridan his mother not to go through his room with great curiosity when he was out. No questions were asked at the bank; he simply went in wearing his best suit and said he wished to open an account, handing over the neat sum of fifty pounds in notes, to start with.

It was all a matter of doing that which was within your scope and not trying for the biggest stuff, but above all working for yourself.

Pickpockets are on the wane now in comparison with Victorian days but there are still pickpockets around and, freelance as he was, after a great number of unsuccessful attempts, he got the knack. It was first a matter of choosing the right circumstances, not clumsily trying to do it on Saturday afternoons in a crowded High Street, for instance, the paterfamilias being, on these occasions, very conscious of his bulging hip pocket. A football match crowd, too, was not as profitable as one might think; folk didn't carry money in bulk when they went to watch the game.

On the other hand, he had had some successful hauls at London Airport, not many but a few large ones, pocket books of flustered travellers from California, seeing to their baggage. The customs counter at Southampton after a big Cunarder had berthed had proved remunerative, too, if one appeared as a porter. Once a drunken old North Country manufacturer whom he had helped as he reeled out of a nude show in Soho had yielded just under three hundred quid.

Four years of hard, grinding experience, with its triumphs and its disappointments, had qualified him for the bigger stuff. All alone, in rubber-soled plimsolls and light clothing with capacious pockets, he had entered and stolen over the years. He felt wise and deeply experienced: observation was what mattered, and the knowledge resulting from this; he felt he could have written a manual, albeit a very, very short one: Axioms for beginners.

> Don't be greedy.
> Start small.
> Make sure it's within your scope.
> Have a careful look round first.
> When you've decided, do it quick.

But the most important of all was the one which, owing to flaws in his character, he abandoned first:

> Do It Alone.

The trouble was that, though he became a master of his art, he did not become master of himself. He indulged.

He did not gratify himself in drugs, or in drink or any other of the vices of the flesh; he allowed himself to enjoy the pleasure of having power over other people much less clever than himself. The same power, which in embryo, he had felt as a cherubic infant with marigold curls. Now that he was no longer a joy to look upon, of such physical perfection that he could make other people do anything he wanted them to do: now that he had been obliged to abdicate that role, he had to cultivate other kinds of magnetism. Thus, in a permissive society which allowed of no adventure in disobedience, no discipline which it was necessary to flout, no thrills in the way of National Service in which one might excel, leaving nothing in fact except a vacuum and the word *bored,* he specialised in the only thrill he could think up, that of leading others into breaking the law, showing them how; demonstrating the exquisite cleverness of robbing and stealing for a livelihood. That's where the *do it alone* adage went, in self-indulgence.

As yet he was not confident enough in his pupils to allow them to take a major role but he was training his little gang of Wotchas in Perfection, with a big P. Though some of them were as old and even older than himself, he was the model upon which they were going to base their future solo efforts. His "Band of Buggers" he called them in his mind and sometimes out loud but secretly and almost tenderly, his "boys"; this only when he was in a good temper.

Entrepreneur was a word with which he had become familiar and it exactly applied to Winston Sledge in that he was a man who ran his own business, and sociological study has recorded that those who run businesses for themselves work harder and strive more to succeed than those working for a master.

It was clever of him, he considered, to take a flat in Fiery Beacon; he had discovered that the best lies are those which most nearly approximate to the truth. Thus one can hide more successfully within a short radius of one's home than in a city hundreds of miles away; if he were noticed coming in or out no one would remember because he would be (sic) a familiar face and/or visiting his parents. He thought the name under which he took the flat exquisitely funny, as well as clever: S. Ledge. He made fools of everybody. Above all, he was, at first, delighted with the choice of girl he had made. She lived only to please, that is, to please her lord and master. This suited Sledge down to the ground. He thoroughly enjoyed the delicious smell of curry which would greet him when he came home to the flat; he enjoyed lying in bed and clapping his hands, as though to a slave, when he required her presence. And most of all he enjoyed making love to her because she never grumbled when he hurt her, but thought it her privilege to be hurt by him.

Of course this, like everything else, became boring in time; at a very early age he had learned from his parents that anything that lasted any length of time at all became boring but after eighteen months he had not yet become so actively bored as to consider a change. Besides, he had not yet found an adequate substitute.

Or had he?

Or had he messed it up by bad temper or by the extremely careless snatching of her handbag and excellent quality hand baggage which he could not resist?

In the manner of an elderly man who feared for the lasting quality of his faculties, he asked himself if he were slipping. His mind must definitely have been elsewhere when he almost automatically pushed her away from the car and drove off with her possessions.

Later in the evening he realised what it had been that distracted him; it was the girl herself. Even though several mornings a week he did a brisk business in pimping, his "home-life" with Amrita, when the day's work was done, had become humdrum.

"How about a bit of class for a change?" he had been asking himself all the way down to Maidenhead when he drove her at 90 mph, on the M4. It would mean a fall in income, of course, because the "class" could be in no way in conjunction with the pimping activities. He considered the possibility of taking yet another flat for the "class" girl but decided against it because it was unwise to increase the weekly expenses when one's income consisted mainly of lump sums collected only by virtue of skill and some luck. No, it would be foolish to increase the amount of rent, electricity and rates which would have to be paid regularly.

It never occurred to him for a moment that the "class" girl would not fall into his arms with a moan of ecstasy; he had never yet come across a girl who had rebuffed him (this was mainly because he had been careful to pick a girl of whom he was pretty sure, first; he couldn't have stood a genuine rebuff).

It wasn't that she was pretty, he told himself, there were lots better-looking girls about, it was just "that she had it written all over her." She must have turned his head because he had driven off with her baggage absent-mindedly, automatically, on the side, as it were. At the time he'd completely forgotten that he had taken her round to the Chelsea dress shop and got her into a job of sorts and of course his chums in the dress shop, high though they had been, couldn't fail to remember by whom she had been introduced to them. It was even possible that she went to the police after he left her on the pavement.

Of course he wasn't too worried about that aspect of it because none of his friends, and that included the hash smokers in "*I Was Napoleon's Mistress*," would split on him.

And naturally, he didn't believe that her name was Frances Smith, it was the kind of very simple name a girl who didn't want her real name known would think up. He would keep an eye on the papers to see if there was a missing heiress.

He prided himself on not "taking a cut off the joint" behind a clump of bushes on the tow-path in Maidenhead; suddenly he was interested in the "gentlemanly" aspect of himself in the presence of a lady. He could become a real gentleman at the drop of a hat, he told himself; he could master the lar-di-dar after a bit of private practice at the driving wheel, with nobody to listen in.

However, the real reason for not taking advantage of the situation on the tow-path at Maidenhead was that he had the Kensington block of flats robbery lined up for the evening and he made it a rule to cut out sex during the hours before he went on a tricky job, thus he kept himself more alert.

But he fancied himself very much, not only in bed with Frances Smith, but married to her, living a bit farther east, which was smart, and voting Conservative.

He went through her handbag and, as he had expected, there was no identification at all, no envelopes, no driving licence, nothing to confirm that she was Frances Smith but enough cash in five-pound notes of pristine freshness to confirm that possibly it was true that she had left home and did not intend to be sent back, would deny strenuously her identity if caught up by the police.

It was Winston-in-Wonderland-Day all right because, when he opened her case, he was thrown. The faint marvellous smell which arose from her possessions entranced him; it was not a voluptuous smell but clean and fresh and delightful, a long way from his experience of a woman's odour. Amrita smelt nice but exotic, faintly musty. In a moment of shocking weakness he buried his face in the clothes, then reverently shut the case without disturbing anything.

Since he could not go back home till the agreed hour of six o'clock, when any male visitors would have left, he drove round and round Chelsea and the better parts of Battersea, looking for her. He went to the coffee bar where he had found her and asked if she had been back; of course she hadn't.

And in this way the Day-to-end-all-days (not quite but getting on that way) wore on until he could go home and have a good meal.

Then there was the evening to be got through, which he did, watching television. He already decided which of his Wotchas he would use this evening, old Joe Bogey, the best of the lot, really. The most reliable. The most unfussy and least nervous, the most steady. The one with whom he had been friends since they were ten. Good old Joe who knew him a lot better than his parents ever had. Anyway, it was his turn.

Like a young husband setting off to work, he bent over his mistress, his beads clashing, to kiss her upon the red caste mark on her forehead; it was his talisman for the moment and he made a habit of kissing it before starting out on a job, for good luck.

And talking about good luck ... before entering the pizza bar he stood outside the side entrance studying the small writing on the nameplate of Madame Joan, Palmist, who practised above. He often had his fortune told, longing always to hear that he would become great. Good fortune was always one step ahead, however; what he particularly wished to know now was that he had already Met His Fate, i.e. his One True Love. Madame Joan, however, did not keep late hours, she went to bed early, as well she might, her hours being the banal ones of 11 a.m. to 5.30 p.m., with time off for lunch; wearing herself out in unselfish occult services to others, it was right that she should have regular meals and a good night's sleep. He would come and see her, perhaps, tomorrow.

He came away with Joe Bogey when the bar closed. He took a taxi home with Joe Bogey. He unlocked his Jag, parked on the north side parking lot. He buttoned himself into his smart new Aquascutum. Joe took off his black sweater and threw it into the back of the car. Joe put on his zipped jacket and his chauffeur's cap, kept under the driving seat. They started off.

They arrived at the Kensington block of flats.

W. Sledge slipped round to the back of the block. He found the ladder amongst the shrubs. He leaned it against the flat roof. He climbed it, on to the small area above the ground floor. He brought out the fresh putty which he kept in a plastic bag in his rainproof pocket and plastered enough of the glass surface for his purposes. He silently crushed a hole in the glass. Putting his arm through, he unhitched the skylight fastening. He pushed up the metal rod holding the frame and slid inside, dropping soundlessly on to the corridor carpet below, thin worn carpet as befitting the retired Indian Army inhabitant of the flat. He nipped across to the living-room, unlocked the door, in which the key had been left, as always, at night. He entered. He went over to the small table. (From his observations in sale rooms he thought it was called a specimen table.) He picked up a cushion and pressed the glass, it broke, not so silently this time. With a tiny pen-torch he chose carefully, rejecting the silver-gilt but picking up the silver: three caddy spoons, five snuff-boxes of varying shapes, all silver, and a big yellow tiger's tooth, silver-mounted, which he would examine later; and finally a silver cigarette-case, gilt carved with a pattern of bamboos, Indian silver most likely, not very valuable but saleable . . . He filled his pockets.

The light went on. She was standing in the doorway pointing a gun at him. She was wearing a red dressing-gown and her hair was obscene with frightful old-fashioned metal curlers. She started to make a speech. He picked up the cushion and went across to her, stuffing it over her face as he held the back of her head, her ghastly curling-pins sticking painfully into the palm of his left hand, even through the kid glove. The gun fell to the ground. He thought of picking it up but didn't touch it. He pressed harder. It wasn't nearly enough; she was struggling like mad; he snatched off the glove of his right hand, holding it in his mouth. He could feel the vomit rising in his throat. He pressed her neck hard where he knew he should press. He put all his strength into it. It happened surprisingly quickly. She went limp as he was holding her. She was as fragile as a bird.

He laid her on the floor, quite gently. Her eyes rolled back. He threw the cushion down on her face. He pulled on the glove. He turned out the light. He left the flat by the front door, which was locked, barred and secured by a chain. He let the Yale lock slide back into place silently as he stood outside. He ran downstairs. He was sick in the hall. He opened the front door and let himself out. He got into his car. The chauffeur drove away from the kerb. He was sick again.

It's me nerves, it's me nerves . . . the first words he learned at Mother's knee. It was curious that when he grew up and understood their implication, they should have fitted so exactly his own case because he wanted to make it quite clear to himself that his frequent vomiting when things went wrong for him was no mere weakness but "me nerves." Years ago, when he'd been young and naturally savage, he had practised strangulation on stray cats in the wilderness beyond World's End; he'd never been sick then. No one could possibly have called him weak (by which he meant, in this context, squeamish).

Young Joe Bogey had got the message all right after the first few moments, he kept his mouth shut; he was frightened, he didn't want to hear how it had gone; he drove home as fast as he dared. When they arrived back at Fiery Beacon he took off his chauffeur's cap, shoved it back under the seat and went off without a word.

Sledge edged himself into the driving seat and shot away in the direction of Walham Green. But on the way he had an idea; slowing down, he felt about with his free hand just touching the back seat and found what he remembered was there: Joe Bogey's pullover. With a flashy swivelling of the driving wheel he turned suddenly in a U turn, backing on his tracks for Kensington and the block of flats he had left so recently. Leaving the car some way down the street he ran silently and swiftly back to the block of flats Nos. 1 to 30, round the side, and in the shrubbery, where he had had the ladder hidden, he dropped the pullover. He also felt he had time to put the ladder back where he had put it two days ago. Soundless and swift, unobtrusive as a rat, he left, a dark shadow in a dark shadowy world.

The receiver lived in one of those streets the houses of which seem only to be a façade because no one is ever seen to be entering or leaving, looking out of the windows, or having things delivered; red brick, they have pale stone facings with simple carvings on the cornices; they have the same colour of unlined curtains in every window in the house, and where at one time there was an aspidistra, now there is a vase of flowers. The acme of respectability.

W. Sledge knew better than to stop at the front door; he left the car at the end of the street and walked down the lane behind the houses, the way the milkmen went. Through the hedge he could see the light on in the house he wanted, the receiver was expecting him, he had been warned by telephone earlier in the day.

He sold his evening's takings to the elderly retired man who had been for most of his lifetime a porter at a big London auctioneers and knew the business "backwards"; knew the antique dealers to whom he could sell the stuff, too. He kept one thing back, he did not know why, it was the tiger's tooth.

Though he came away with his pocket-book pleasantly full his nerves were still jangling. He knew he must sell the car, which had served him well but which he must part with because he had had it long enough for it to be associated with him even by someone who wasn't observant. "Yes," anybody who knew him would agree, "W. Sledge has this dark green Jag."

It would have to go . . . and quickly. But first he went to his flat where he was again sick. He did not stay long. Amrita was uneasy, he left after having a bit of a rest in his sitting-room.

Unfortunately the firm who would buy it, who dealt in cars with a shady past, would not be open for business till eight o'clock. This garage was situated in a wilderness of similar establishments on the Southend Road; they had a piece of empty ground the size of four tennis-courts on which the cars were lined up with the price written in white paint on the windscreen, the whole surrounded by a string of gay coloured electric light bulbs. It remained floodlit all night, too, so that the night-watchman could see if any pilfering were taking place.

Since sleep was not possible, he drove straight there and walked up and down the lines of cars, rejecting each one in his mind until dawn came and he could go a few yards down the road to a good pull-up for car men, where he had breakfast and began to feel better. He had a chat about cars with an articulated-truck driver who said he was saving up for a Rover 2000.

The salesman, who knew him well and had sold him the Jag, was perfectly prepared to take it back on part exchange and no questions asked.

"There's nothing in that lot I want," Sledge said with an almost audible sneer towards the lines of cars displayed.

"What do you fancy, then?" the salesman asked with biting sarcasm, "a Porsche, eh?"

"A Rover 2000!"

"He he he!" giggled the salesman, "settling down, are you? Looking for something class?"

"I told you what I want," Sledge returned sternly.

"Don't make me laugh, I've got a cracked lip," the salesman begged. He sobered up almost at once because the boss arrived and immediately offered Sledge his own Rover 2000; it had done a big mileage but the engine number had been successfully eliminated and there were new number-plates available. It was a treat of a car, he said, responds to the touch like a glorious sexy bird, Cleopatra couldn't do no better.

The hocus pocus and abracadabra over insurance and log book would make an interesting handbook of the Hints to Conjurors variety (All Done With Mirrors): it took time, however, and finally, after a lapse of several hours, W. Sledge drove back westwards, the owner of a different car from the one in which he had driven down the Southend Road; dead white and by no means the burglar's favourite make. It was a bold stroke and his first (alas, his only) move up the social ladder.

It was a gruelling day though, waiting for the news to break and when final editions of the evening papers appeared, though he had been expecting it, the news of the Kensington widow's cruel death almost winded him with shock.

With a tankful of petrol he had been driving about all day, not going anywhere he was known; trying out his car on the M1; having a meal at Luton, then back to London and round and round Regent's Park, past the Zoo three times, hoping to catch the eye of a "bird," but there were few people about on foot.

Finally, the evening paper . . . and then there was no time to be lost.

CHAPTER VI

Receivers who are not to be trusted are no good to anybody; but receivers have their own ethics and their own rules and these they make clear to their clients before taking them on, if they have any sense or pride. This particular elderly receiver in Walham Green had worked for many years as the trusted employee of a famous auctioneer but he had not failed to observe the awful crooks some apparently impeccable dealers were; clever as a bag of monkeys, he would say, they always got away with it. So in his retirement this old porter got his own back on all the years of watching other people's successful, adroit manoeuvring and did a quiet overnight business in relieving burglars of their loot and re-selling it to very okay customers.

"But armed robbery or robbery with violence and you've had it," he would say over and over again to his feeders, making quite sure they did not forget it or think that over the years he had relaxed the rule. He could not and would not put up with any hint of violence whatsoever, he did not like it.

He did not buy an evening paper but he saw the details of the Kensington murder next morning all right. It wasn't the first time he had gone to the nearest police station; they knew him and had a strange relationship with him because he had been immensely useful to them in the past.

There was a kind of involuted code of honour between them; in exchange for their not actually asking questions of him, he might give them any information he had regarding armed robberies and violence. He disposed of his purchases so very quickly, within hours, so the actual goods were never on his premises for long and an arrest wasn't possible unless stolen goods were found in his possession. The police knew neither his name nor his address but they could easily have found it out had they wished. They trusted him to come to them if there were any violence suspected. Furthermore they knew that he dealt only in small stuff; anything as big as a tankard or a teapot was out.

The receiver did not know either W. Sledge's name or his address but W. Sledge, upset as he was, had made a small mistake when he had called; he had unaccountably taken off the dark raincoat he was wearing in order to empty the pockets which were weighing him down, and the receiver had observed his attire with great interest: the tight trousers, the orange-coloured thin polo-necked sweater, the thick fisherman's knit pullover ... and above all, the strings of beads hanging round his neck. Lots of young men wore beads, everybody knew, but the receiver had thought it a damn' silly thing to go on a robbery with all that junk round your neck: suppose one of the strings had broken, been left upon the scene of the crime?

"Too clever by half, I hope you get him, he's a cocky youngster," the receiver ended, and the Chief Inspector courteously called him Sir when he thanked him as the old man left his office, even though he had told him nothing about the articles received but simply offered a description of a young man's appearance in a possible connection with the Kensington murder.

"Dad?"

Pa Bogey slept so lightly that he seemed never to be asleep. "Yes, son?" He pressed the bedside light switch which lay in bed alongside him so that little movement was necessary to turn it on. Joe blinked at the sudden light; he went over to the window, looking down on the mist-shrouded space which was river, his back to his father so that his face was not visible to the prostrate man.

"When's Mum coming back?"

"Should have been today, I was expecting a tinkle all evening. I hope nothing's gone wrong."

Joe ran his tongue round his dry lips; in taking his father into his confidence he was doing the inconceivable; he had been driven to it for reasons which he deplored in himself, motives for which he was ashamed; they did not fit in with his idea of himself, a tough-guy.

"It's like this ..." In a spasmodic series of gasps and gulps, of hesitations and evasions, he managed to get it out.

There was a kid, a girl that is, in trouble, derelict, *no* not derelict ... destitute, that was it, destitute. Nowhere to go, not a penny piece to her name; last night ... it had been late, too late to disturb him, he'd, that is,

he'd borrowed Mum's bed to put her in, like, just for the night. But now
tonight she was still around. As Mum hadn't come home . . . that is, like
. . . he thought it a good idea to put her in Mum's bed again.

This, Pa Bogey assured him, was quite okay. He did not add that he
knew perfectly well that Mum's bed had been occupied the night before
and that it was his opinion that it had been occupied by Joe as well . . .
however . . .

Joe was having great difficulty in conveying what he wished to convey,
he wasn't used to taking his father into his confidence, in fact it was the
very last thing he wished to do but there was no other way out of it.

This evening he had taken the girl to the pizza bar and it had been
agreed with Silas d'Ambrose that she should act as assistant, probationer
as Silas called it, in the bar for a nominal (again Silas's word) wage, for
the time being. That so-called nominal wage was not enough to keep
her anywhere in London, so . . . if she could stay here, with the Bogeys,
for a short period, it would be a great help.

"Yes, son, I daresay your Mum would agree."

He did not ask where Joe would sleep when Mum was home again
and Joe knew that the true answer hung upon that question.

"I can doss down in the living-room," he mumbled.

"You wouldn't be having her in your bed, then," his father murmured
thoughtfully, a statement rather than a question.

"She's not that kind of girl."

"Cripes!" his father exclaimed, taken by surprise (saying afterwards,
unrealistically, that you could have knocked him down with a "fevver").
"What do you call her then?"

"Frances Smith."

"Sweet Fanny Adams," his father murmured thoughtfully, and Joe got
the message. He felt a sudden, horrifying, irresistible rush of emotion.

But not on any account was Joe's Dad going to ask another question,
to have done so would have been to break the spell. Parents would
always ask questions and that was where they went wrong, in Joe's
Dad's opinion. He very much wanted to know where Miss Frances
Smith now was; since it was well after midnight, he felt almost certain
she was already in Mrs. Bogey's bed but he said nothing and whistled
very faintly through his teeth as he used to when his hands were
occupied in work of some kind and he wished it to be known that he

couldn't care less what had been, or was being, told him. So Joe told him all the rest of it.

He stared up at the ceiling, still whistling faintly, and let the flood pour over him.

There was a long pause after Joe had finished. The boy had turned to face him as he had been talking, and now he was resting his behind on the edge of the window-sill, his back to the marvellous night view.

Joe's father had not always been as clever and wise; but as he always reminded himself, it's the handicapped folk who manage to achieve what they would not have otherwise done, like the man without hands who carves the Lord's Prayer on a walnut. *He that overcometh* . . . Joe's Dad had had a long time to do nothing but think and if his body was entirely useless, his brain and mind were not. He had worked out a philosophy of his own.

He said: "Well. Joe, you've got yourself in a real old hash but it is what was to be expected; you've only followed the trend. This may not be the first time you've bust the law, not by a long chalk, but it'll be the first time you've been, or are going to be, found out, bound to be, as I see it, they'll catch up on young Sledge and he's not going to shield you, that's for sure!"

The kindness of his tone was somehow unbearable; Joe prayed that he was not going to cry, though he was very near it; he sniffed loudly a great many times and thus kept his cheeks dry.

"It's obvious what you're going to do, this time, son, eh?"

Joe nodded, wordless.

"You were an . . . what they call, accessory. If you'd set out with a gun, or if he'd set out with a gun, to do that robbery and the old lady had got herself shot: well, I reckon you'd be in it as bad as young Sledge. But I can't help thinking there's a chance, that as you didn't set out with guns, you may be all right, you I mean, not Sledge. What did you say, Joe?"

He had made a croaking sound which had something to do with the word loyalty.

"Yes," his father agreed, " 'Honour amongst thieves' but it don't say anything about 'honour among murderers,' do it?"

He began to feel much better, having told his father everything was a blessed relief, somehow or other; he almost felt that perhaps he was going to struggle out of this mess-up still himself, if a different one in that he would not be in any way attached to W. Sledge and his gang in future.

"There's just one thing," he said slowly, and even his voice had changed, "what's going to happen when I go to the police," he jerked his head, "to her?"

"I'd have to have a look at her before I could say."

"I mean ... when I go to the police tomorrow ... they might keep me there; she'll have to know where I am and all that, otherwise she might think I'd stood her up, eh?"

Joe's Dad was frowning, not sure how to reply. He was certain she was a bitch of a girl, predatory and probably pregnant. Joe surprised him by saying, as though he were throwing a final spanner in the works:

"She's not our class."

His Dad made such a wry face that Joe could not help smiling.

"Up, not down!" he said. "Her Dad's a Lord somethink or other."

"A lord?"

"Not exactly, he don't sit in the House of Lords, he's a plain Mister but with a ... that is, he has two names and he's called by both and he's a big gun in the county, sort of thing."

"That makes a lot of difference, I suppose ..."

"Aye, it does," Joe returned with feeling, "she's got to be treated proper."

"I see," his Dad returned, though bewildered.

Joe said there was something else he had better tell him; his Dad had had just about as much as he could take for one go but said, "Go on, chum!"

"Sledge has what he calls an establishment of his own."

"Oh, yea?"

"He has a flat of his own and he keeps an Indian mistress, very smooth, has done for pretty near two years. She ... he sends chaps to her, daytime, get it?"

"Part-time prostitute?"

Joe nodded soberly.

Joe's Dad clicked his tongue as though it was a pity. "It was better when it was on the streets, open and above board, the good old prostitute mincing along Shaftesbury Avenue with a tiny dog, her bum wagging from side to side ... oh, for the good old days!"

Joe looked disapproving, even slightly shocked.

"The thing is, Dad, you've got to know this, since you're getting to know the lot. It's here!"

"How do you mean, here?"

"Here in this block of flats. Fiery Beacon."

"Get away!"

"It's over the other side, north entrance, seventeenth floor, looking out over Hampstead way ... He's got it in the name of S. Ledge ..."

Joe's Dad couldn't laugh properly, he made the choking rather sad sound denoting laughter and Joe waited calmly till it was over.

"Such a pity, such a pity," Joe's Dad gasped at last, "all that skill gone to waste."

"It's not gone to waste. Dad, he's making a good income, two thousand this year shouldn't wonder, tax-free; it's the chaps that work for themselves that makes the money, I know that for sure. If I didn't know that I'd never of had nothink to do with Sledge."

"You 're not working for yourself if you're working for Sledge."

"No, but don't you see? That rake-off I get every time I help him, it's all saving up."

His Dad nodded, "I see all right."

"So's I can have my own pizza bar, the idea was; I worked it out; I've a bit put by already. Silas d'Ambrose is not that old and he's doing very nicely thanks, can take sixty quid a night at the weekends, easy. I've planned a lot better show than his ..." he paused, "only it's all over now."

There was a long silence.

"So it's over to you. Dad, if you look after Frances I'll do the rest, eh?"

"I ain't said I'll look after Frances," Joe's Dad observed, "since I've not clapped an eye on her. I might not like her, how about that, eh?"

"You'll like her all right, Dad."

Though Joe had had more than enough of this haunted, long-drawn-out day, it seemed years away from this time last night when he was squatting on the roof trying to work out things, hoping that his instinct about Sledge's activities in the Kensington flat had been imagination.

As he left his father's room he heard a kind of rat-scratching on the flat door. "Christ," Sledge gasped when Joe opened it and looked out. Joe very much did not wish to see Sledge either at this moment or ever again but he also did not wish Frances Smith, now in his mother's bed and, he hoped, asleep, to be awakened by an argument. He stepped outside, pinning back the latch, and shut the door too, after him. The wet warm wind blew in his face.

"I knew you'd got home, I watched you come in," Sledge snarled. "What the hell are you doing with that bird?"

"Get out of here," Joe returned uncompromisingly.

Alas, alas! The gutter rats and the Sledges will always win in a contest of wits with those more simple. First he brought out a bundle of folded banknotes and, looking very straightly and honestly at Joe, he handed it to him. "What I owe you for last night . . ."

"Gettaway with it!" and Joe struck the offending notes out of his hand; they fell on to the wet concrete, narrowly escaping being tossed over the wall into space.

"What's the good of that?" Sledge wondered, but he couldn't resist bending down and picking them up. "Come clean, have you? Don't want to touch the tainted money . . . Phew, you're bright yaller . . ."

"I never promised to help in murder!"

Sledge clicked his tongue, shocked. "That's a nasty word."

"How could you be such a bloody fool?"

"It was the old lady was the bloody fool; she was going to shoot me."

"Good for her, I wish she had . . ."

"She was a dangerous lunatic. I didn't mean to hurt her, I was just trying to shut her up; she began screaming; I pressed a cushion against her mouth to stop her. How could I help it when she fell apart in my hands?" He looked at Joe, hands widely spread, like the domestic help who had accidentally broken the best teapot.

But Joe had no intention of arguing with him on the strip of balcony outside his parents' flat, or anywhere else. He backed to the front door, not wishing to turn his back on Sledge, for a definite reason.

"Wait a minute." Sledge darted round the corner, out of sight and reappeared almost immediately with a luxurious-looking zippered piece of hand baggage and a pigskin handbag. He bowed slightly: "The property of your friend Miss Smith, who was out with me yesterday afternoon." He put a world of lasciviousness into his leer, heavy with innuendo. "Yes, we went to Maidenhead. Oh, what a loverly bird! I was pitched, really I was; forgot meself so far as to drive off with her possessions; been wondering how I could get them back to her and blow me! In you come with the self-same loverly piece . . ."

"Shut up!" Joe hissed. He snatched up the baggage and threw it behind him, into the flat. "Now eff off," he begged.

But Sledge had no intention of leaving; he leaned back comfortably against the wall and said he was going to the police tomorrow to tell them the whole story.

"It's just a matter of who'll get there first," Joe returned.

"Not at all, not at all. I've no record, remember; it's my story vee yours. It's more like you killed her and I did the driving, since it's my car; you're a bigger chap altogether, hefty, stronger physically."

"There's nothing to pin it on me, nothink at all."

"Isn't there?"

"Of course there isn't . . ."

"Except, where's your black wool pullover, the one you were wearing when you left work?"

After one paralysed moment Joe attacked him, unwisely. He had often rushed at him in desperation when he goaded, over the years since they were both boys in the playground; once Sledge had lost his temper and hurt him very badly in the crutch and since that occasion Joe had been more wary. Sledge lost his temper now and a hideous situation developed when it appeared that he was trying to throw Joe over the wall to drop twenty-one stories on to the concrete forecourt below. There was an iron handrail along the top of the wall, bringing the lifting necessary to throw over anyone or any bulky thing to the awkward height of five feet; Joe clung to this rail with both hands and instinctively remembering the crutch kick he had once received he fought back like a mad thing, his legs flailing wildly, one kick arriving on target and knocking Sledge double with groans of agony.

Joe quickly slid inside his own front door, slammed it, and sank down, breathless, crying but turning his sobs to gasps when he realised Frances was kneeling beside him and thin cries of anxiety were coming from his father's room.

So finally Frances was introduced to Joe's father in a manner very far from the way Joe would have wished and the noise of banging and kicking on the front door distracting them all three.

"Has the chap gone mad?" Joe's Pa wanted to know. "Sounds darn like it to me; you'd best ring up the police now, Joe lad."

Being an outside door fairly exposed to the elements it was stronger than it would otherwise have been; it withstood Sledge's attack and by the time Joe had pulled himself together enough to call the police to restrain the madman, there was an ominous silence.

"He's thrown himself over and a damn' good thing," Joe's father said out loud.

Joe could barely stand up, his legs would not keep steady enough for him to convey himself to the telephone or even to much-needed bed. He had felt himself to be hanging in space for a few appalling seconds though he had not in fact been as near to it as that; he felt he could never again go out of his own front door without turning sick and dizzy. If he had been one who was afraid of heights he would never have been able to live contentedly in Fiery Beacon, but he suddenly became conscious of the terrifying height of their home above the ground.

When he sat up on the roof in "his place" he enjoyed the slight perceptible swing as though the whole building were swaying, when there was a strong wind; the feeling was not so imaginary because it did sway slightly but now his semi-circular canals had been upset and were behaving as though they had been put in a centrifuge. He was, in fact, feeling the actual symptoms of sea-sickness and he remained sitting on the floor in the hall, head down between his knees, whilst Miss Frances Smith made friends with his father, giving the reasons for her presence in a series of alarming headlines.

" . . . so that is how I come to be here, Mr. Bogey, and thank you very much for allowing it."

"That's all right," Joe's father said comfortably, "what's worrying me now is this chap Sledge. I saw him often as a boy, always coming into this flat; hasn't been here so much recently; I never took to him but our Joe admired him, copied him and all that."

"The thing is," Frances explained, "he's got magnetism; it's not that he's good-looking or charming; in fact, I think he's ugly, and his hair that ghastly colour! But he's colourful, his clothes and all those beads; and then he's confident and bossy; gives you the idea that he's in with 'everybody' whoever that is. I quite understand how Joe felt about him, look at me! I've fallen into the same trap! But I can't understand why he's brought my baggage back, and un-touched!"

CHAPTER VII

Madame Joan, Palmist, did not exactly live for her work; she had so many troubles of her own that she could attend to those of her customers with only half her mind, some of the time. Indeed, there were times when her blonde receptionist stood in for her.

When she had time she would grumble at the small amount she charged, only ten shillings and sixpence with an extra five shillings for telling the same things all over again in cards, "confirming her findings" was what she called this. She often boasted that she could set up in Harley Street and earn six guineas for half an hour of listening to people talking about themselves, if only someone would lend her the money to get started there. As it was, she earned quite a good living as a poor man's psychiatrist, mostly amongst foreigners, occasionally wild characters from the North, in London for football matches, and she also had a small group of regulars who came every week or every month for guidance.

Most of her customers took it for granted that she had supernatural powers, that she switched over to "the Fates" once the ten-and-sixpence had crossed her palm. But the interesting thing about her was that she did, in fact, have second sight, or the perfectly natural phenomenon of extrasensory perception, *when she was concentrating*. Though she couldn't have cared less whether she had this or not, it was a fact that three generations of women before her, her mother, grandmother and great-grandmother had been "Fortune Tellers," and the extra-sensory perception which lies dormant in everyone (only occasionally stirring, to the disbelief of all) can react to continued stimulus. She would hand out all the usual patter about tall, dark strangers and journeys abroad and then, if she were in the least interested in the person sitting before her and they happened to be listening anxiously, she might come up with something to which it was really worth listening. The strange thing was that her customers hardly ever realised this; they would, if they went to her for more than "the giggle," remember, later on, that what was now happening to them had been foretold them by that fortune teller they went to in Soho, but as fortune-telling was the woman's profession and as they had paid their fee it aroused no surprise or surmise.

There was one vitiating snag in Madame Joan's supernatural powers, she never knew whether the information she actually received referred to the past or to the future, unless, of course, it was something to do with her customer's death.

Only her regular customers, having nothing better to do, called in the mornings as a rule. She was therefore surprised that a young man should call shortly after her advertised time of opening. Her daughter, being a hairdresser, and not yet left for work, was in the process of taking out her mother's rollers after drying her hair; she showed the customer into the consulting room and, returning to the bathroom, helped Madame Joan to put on the splendid black lace mantilla which she always wore with great effect, the lacy edge pulled well down over her eyes, to make them look mysterious.

The fee paid, Madame Joan leaned across the purple silk tablecloth embroidered with gold thread and took both her customer's hands, looking at him with as much interest as she could muster at this time of day. His hair was really a shocking colour; in a crowd he would stand out like a carrot-coloured flag; marvellous in a girl but a disadvantage in a young man, possibly.

"Oh, dear me," she exclaimed, bent over his palm, "oh dear oh dear oh dear!" W. Sledge stirred irritably. She was silent for so long after that first outburst that he couldn't help snapping nervously: "Well, get on with it!" Her head flew up, her lips retracted. "Have patience, young man," she reproved. She placed his hands flat on the table, palms upwards, and studied first one, then the other. She turned them over and looked at the back of his hands for so long that he broke out into a nervous sweat.

"Well, I never!" she exclaimed.

And then, after an unbearable length of time, she poured out the usual mechanical lingo; there was the dark girl, of course.

"Do you see any other girl?"

"Oh yes, my dear, I see a girl, but strangely mixed up somehow . . ." she tailed off vaguely. After a moment or two she went on: "I think I ought to warn you to be careful."

"In what way?"

"You're in some danger . . ."

He wriggled forward excitedly in his chair. "What kind of danger?"

"I'm not sure, another five shillings and the cards might be able to tell me something more."

Out came the five shillings and out came the cards; she flipped them professionally, to and fro; she handed them to him and asked him to shuffle and cut; she studied them carefully.

"I see a beautiful, rich young lady," she said in her old professional whine, swinging away into the usual ambiguities, and when she had finished she sat with her hands folded on the table in front of him and stared at him.

"But remember," she went on dreamily now, "all is not gold that glitters."

"How do you mean?" he snapped back.

"You are in danger, you know; fortune and success apart, you're in danger, so I'd take care if I were you."

"This young girl you mentioned, how do you know she's rich?"

"I can see a motor car," she murmured huskily, "a beautiful long white motor car and this girl . . ."

"You're getting mixed up," he chuckled, pleased, interrupting her, which was perhaps a pity, in the light of what happened later. "That's my car you see; just bought it!"

"Oh, is it?" She was losing interest now. "I'm afraid your time's up now, can you find your way out?"

"Well, ta a lot." He stood up and walked to the door.

She relented: "Now mind what I said, you've been warned . . . about the danger, I mean."

"Okay, and ta again!" he called over his shoulder. He seemed in a hurry to go now.

As Madame Joan's daughter finished off her mother's hair-do her mother said: "Funny that; I would swear those hands had been or are going to strangle someone."

"Who? Young or old?" The girl went on with her job; talking over her cases if they had been in the least interesting was quite a normal occurrence with her mother.

"I didn't see *who,* I didn't actually *see* anything except a big white car. I knew he'd tried to strangle somebody with those hands, that's all, or will do."

"Well, how about ringing the police?"

"What's the good of that?"

"The public are asked to help in the crime thing, heard it on the telly last night ..."

"I don't know whether he has already strangled somebody or he's going to strangle somebody; besides, if I did, it's got to happen or it has happened, I can't stop it even if I knew who he is and who he's going to strangle; if it hasn't happened it's *got* to happen, it's there, written in the air ..."

But the noise from the lacquer-spray being used liberally on her newly set hair drowned her words and her daughter was no longer listening anyway.

"My girl can't stand the colour of my hair," he told the barber three streets away.

"What you bin doin' to her?" the barber asked, fingering the stuff which was, in fact, a deeper shade than carrots.

"That's what she says, anyway."

"I could bleach it," the barber suggested unrealistically.

"Cor! I'd look a right Charlie ..."

"Albino's the word," the barber said helpfully, "I've a coupla those as customers; why not try a nice pale albino? makes a change; only you ain't pink-eyed to match."

"You're pulling my leg as well as my hair," W. Sledge snapped irritably.

"It's only ... well, you got pale skin to match your hair, like, I mean your skin kind of goes with your hair, see what I mean?"

"Well, I'm not going to parade around as no effing albino just to please you," W. Sledge shouted.

"A nice rich black, then," the barber agreed hurriedly, "but don't blame me ..."

"Get on with it, man!" W. Sledge urged.

And now, unconsciously, W. Sledge's walk, though it did not actually change, took on characteristics it had not shown previously; it became more purposeful, verging on a swagger. Not that he, or anyone else he knew, walked much, but there was always the long and longer walk from where one had to park the car if he couldn't leave it in his usual underground dive; they were careful about their parking, W. Sledge and those of his ilk; parking-fine tickets can lead to magistrates' courts and from there if you were not careful to police courts; it was wiser, if much more difficult, to park carefully.

It's like this, he might well have argued; if you strangle an old, old lady ... either it gets you down and you crawl to the nearest police station, flat on your face ... or you don't; if you don't, you've got to rise above it. And if you do rise above it, you're way up there, you've got this feeling you're top brass, that is, you're above others; you're on your own and you've got to act like you're somebody. Act? Well, it's not that much acting either; you *are* somebody.

That, in fairly simple language, was the way it worked with W. Sledge, anyway.

He had not, of course, seriously meant going to the police, which he had threatened Joe Bogey with this morning; he had hoped Joe would not be at home so that he could graciously return the cases to the young lady, whom he knew to be sheltering in Joe's flat, because he had watched from his car for Joe's return home; giving them back to her as though he had chanced upon them and was doing her a favour. Joe's manner infuriated him: perfectly ready to help in a spot of crime when there was no danger, only the pleasure of driving the car and getting well paid for it. But the minute there was a spot of bother he acted scared; much too chummy with those parents of his; they'd talk him into going to the police easy. It was a near thing; he'd been so angry he really had been going to chuck Joe over, only he was so heavy, he couldn't get him up over the handrail, that was the trouble. Anyway, he hoped he'd scared Joe out of any informing nonsense, and thus he brooded on his way back to the car and home from the West End.

With his now temporarily smooth, dull, lacquered black head, wearing the only suit he possessed, a tight black affair, the sleeves much too short, the suit he would have worn for the old lady's funeral, had he attended it, he strode back to where he had carefully left at a meter his white car and drove home to Fiery Beacon, parking it in a different position from usual.

The lifts did not start from an indoor entrance hall but from a concrete paving, sheltered from the skies but definitely out-of-doors. This had often annoyed W. Sledge and he had promised himself, one of these days, to move to a "luxury flat," possibly one which had a jazzy carpet in the entrance hall and mirror-lined walls, where he could lounge about, admiring his reflection and smoking, whilst waiting for the lift, instead of standing in a moist draught in a puddle of water where the concrete was slightly worn.

Arriving at the seventeenth floor, too, he would have preferred it if he had stepped out on to thick carpet, inserted his key into a lush, flush door rather than step across more concrete which often meant avoiding puddles even up there and putting his key into the lock of his front door whilst rain was blown down the back of his neck.

However, an end to all this was in sight at last.

It was satisfactory that Amrita should utter a high thin scream and gather her bosoms together in terror at the new look of him; it was slightly less pleasing when, having finally recognised her lord and master, she should walk round him, her face showing extreme distaste.

"Oh, my man!" (as she had been instructed to call him), "what have you done with yourself?"

"Get out of my sight!" he snarled and, going through to the bedroom, he looked for and found, where they had been tidied away, the clothes he had worn the night before last, the orange polo-necked jersey, the fisherman's knit pull-over, the jeans ... the beads. He ranged round, looking for a brown paper carrier.

"But why do you ...?"

"What ...?"

"Please, my man ..."

With each of these small sorties he brushed her off. "If you start to be a nuisance ... finish!" he told her sternly. At which, of course, she sat down and cried.

"Is anyone coming today?" she managed through her sniffing and tears.

"No ... no! That's all over, no more brothel-stuff, it doesn't pay."

"But it does, you have said so many, many times. It pays! It pays the rent, you have said, and the rates, you have said, and the electricity, you have said. Otherwise, you have said many times, if I did not work during the day I could not stay here in this flat and have the electric fires on all day long. I have to earn my keep, you have said ..." Her voice rose to a thin eastern whine.

"Look, it's over, don't you understand, that part of it is *over,* o, vee, ee, ar!"

She stared at him with her strange eyes which were chocolate drops, plain and simple, there being no discernible difference in texture or colour between the iris and pupil. He had thought it many a time but had considered it would be impolite to say so; now he didn't care whether he was impolite or not.

He stared at her with distaste and rudely said: "Chocolate drops!" out loud.

She gave an extended edition of her former wail; she had now fully received the message and it was one she had received before, from other men; she was being shaken off, stood up, ditched, given the push. She knew an Indian girl called Push-Pam whose name had given much amusement amongst the boys. Push-Pam had cried very much in a "Ladies" once when Amrita had found her there, and had explained to Amrita the joke of her name: ". . . and I get pushed out always, in the end . . .!" she had screamed hysterically.

It was so much worse for an Indian girl to get pushed out than for a European girl; her family would never receive her back; her father would announce that he wished her dead rather than back home after living with any man as his wife without a ceremony.

"I understand, I understand," she moaned, "I am just another Push-Pam!"

"Oh shut up, shut up!" W. Sledge cried, shouting down the tiny Calvinist inside him screaming to get out. "What do you mean, anyway, 'just another Push-Pam'?" he couldn't help asking.

"You're pushing me out and where am I to go?"

"A young beauty like you won't take long getting fixed up again. Go to the club or something!"

"You don't understand . . ."

"No, I don't. You've had all these chaps coming along to make love to you. Don't any of them want a lot more of it?" he asked crudely.

"I belong to you, to you!" she cried on a dying fall.

"Not any more, you don't!" W. Sledge was looking thoughtfully at the soles of the elastic-sided boots he had worn the night before last in Kensington and had wiped barely clean. They would have to go, too; they would have left quite a distinctive dent in the soil of the shrubbery where he had hidden the ladder. What a lot to be thought of, and that girl moaning and creating . . . it was enough to drive anyone up the pole. Push-Pam, indeed! Not a bad idea, if it came to the point.

"Push-Pam, indeed!" he said as he rummaged about the bedroom: "All girls like you get the push in the end, didn't you know?"

She was silent now, hard, hard chocolate drops looking at him in horror.

"Where the hell is that carrier?" he shouted at last. "That brown one we've had for months?"

She said nothing, only stared.

He came close to her and thrust his face up so that it was nearly touching hers: "Where is it, where is it, *where is it?*"

"So you really are going to push me out?" she murmured in a low voice.

"Well . . ." he gesticulated vaguely that that was what he had in mind.

"But where do I go?"

"I don't know!"

" . . . you don't know . . ." she repeated drearily.

"Look, you're probably a lot older than I am . . ."

"You know I'm not . . ."

"You look it."

"I can't help that, you didn't think so when I came here, eighteen months ago. If I now look aged it is because you have sent me so many men, to wear me out. And you yourself have worn me out, with your terrible tempers!"

"Well, that's your look-out, isn't it, I mean . . ." he shrugged.

"You've changed," she wept.

He had turned away and was continuing his search, indifferent to her pleading, her murmuring, her complaints, her whining. He had to be, he forced himself to be: impervious.

"All right," she said quietly, "I shall have to tell, I shall have to tell what I know, my man; if I have to leave here I have nowhere to go, nowhere I can lay my head down. I can only go to the police station, they may be kind, they may send me to . . . to a welfare centre. I'm only fourteen!" (Though she had, in fact, become fifteen some months ago.)

W Sledge felt his blood congealing. Of course . . . of course . . . of course; the old cliché, though he did not form the words because he did not know them, but the general gist came to him for the first time in his short life: *hell knoweth no fury like a woman scorned.*

Her death was suddenly legalised, it was as though she had, with bowed head, willingly agreed to her own end. Indeed—suggested it.

Though he did not realise it, he now worked slowly, his actions retarded by an incipient sadness. She followed him about.

"So it's blackmail, is it?" he said once and she did not answer. Slowly he took a tool out of the kitchen drawer, prised up the carpet behind their bed, pulled up a floor board and, feeling around with his hand he brought out a fairly big wad of notes, peeled off an amount which he counted carefully, replaced the rest, put down the carpet, hammered in the tacks exactly as they had been, pushed the bed back into place and all the time she was watching him, following him back into the kitchen. It did not matter now that she knew where he hid his fortune, that is, all that he did not put into a bank.

He found some writing paper on the pad he sometimes used, an envelope, a ball-point pen. He wrote to the rent-collecting department of the council, he told them he was going away for three months and enclosed the rent for the period; the envelope was bulgy, he licked the flap and, turning it over, he banged the back of it with his fist, looking up into her agonised face, challengingly. Triumphantly he brought out a fivepenny stamp which he had remembered to buy.

"Blackmail," he repeated. "You wicked girl," he shook his head sadly, "I am ashamed of you!"

Unaccountably but as though prolonging his time with her, he started to tidy up the little kitchen, which was, in fact, not untidy. He cleared whatever dishes there were off the table and put them in the sink. With his back turned to her he gave her one more chance.

"You could go now," he said clearly, "you could walk out of that door and go down in the lift and I should never see you again, that is, if you would forget you ever lived with me. I must, I must be on my own ... you understand?"

She was so silent that he looked round to see if she was still there, she moved so quietly, gliding rather than walking, an indoor girl, a girl for the bedchamber only, unpractical, unintelligent, discardable, or was it, disposable? That was it, everything useful or useless should be *disposable*, these days. The useful always became useless in time.

Chocolate drops ...

"Why don't you go?" he suggested. "I should, if I was you."

She stood silent, staring.

He peered out of the window above the sink. "A nice day, at last!" he said. He walked past her into the tiny hall, he turned and clapped his hands: "Come!"

Stiffly, but gliding still, she went to him as though sleep walking. He opened the entrance door which was both front and back door. The sun was beginning to burn the smoky fog off the city all round, no sun shone on their entrance balcony because the flat faced north, looking across to Hampstead. She had lived only to please him, her instinct was still to please, never to resist, always to please.

He said "Come!" and clapped his hands for the last time. What could she do other than obey, if only to please him?

Nobody heard the high, thin scream as she fell.

But everybody on that side of Fiery Beacon heard the shouts, the roars, the cries, the screams of terror from young S. Ledge, who chose to run the whole way down the seventeen flights of concrete stairs rather than wait for the lift; as though there was anything he could do when he arrived at ground level. He was so dizzy from the effort that he allowed himself to fall to the ground, lying face downwards, shouting his lungs to bits. They ran to help him rather than her, what lay on the ground was beyond help; nobody wanted to look anyway.

Only one brave old man tore off the art-silk bedspread he had just been pulling neatly into place over his bed, ran out and covered the obscenity lying there on the concrete.

Someone rushed to the telephone box, someone else ran for the nearest policeman, several people held out friendly arms to the bereaved boy who seemed to be retching his heart out; they almost struggled between themselves to take him into their homes, to give him brandy or cups of tea, to comfort him. To help.

"Push-Pam," he babbled wildly, "her name was Push-Pam!"

The evening paper carried a small paragraph: "Girl falls to death from tower block" and that was all. Three days later, after the inquest, the local paper carried a somewhat longer story but the episode was too ordinary to be of much interest to their readers; the whole thing was almost too clear-cut and simple. The man Mr. Sam Ledge, aged 22, with whom she had been living for eighteen months, did not even know her surname; or perhaps had heard it at some time but could not remember, even if he could pronounce it. He had suddenly to go abroad for three months "on business" and the girl had threatened to kill herself when he had told her he could not take her.

When she saw him actually putting the three months' rent in advance into an envelope she had realised that he meant what he had said, that he was making no arrangements for her during that period, and at the thought of being left alone she became hysterical. When he had at last believed that she was comforted, she slipped out and threw herself over the balcony wall.

One more unfortunate . . .

The neighbours knew nothing about the couple but the caretakers knew that she was a prostitute who received men in the flat during the day, when the man with whom she lived was "out at work." No relative came forward; nothing was said about her age, no one seemed to know it. The status of prostitutes having been severely devalued in recent times, the coroner really was not very interested.

S. Ledge, much to his disgust, was described as an "out-of-work" labourer.

It was so very obviously suicide, or in common parlance: "just one of those things . . ."

S. Ledge felt sad when, back home in his flat, he opened the drawers that had been Amrita's and saw her neatly folded saris; he did not know what he was going to do with them, but somehow, for the moment, he did not wish even to see them.

Something was happening to him; you can't murder two people in one week and go on being the same person inside. He could not have described the feelings he had in words, he thought only that he felt very much better for the happenings; he felt very distinctly that he was "on his way"; that he was pressing on to bigger things, not words but today's terms covering such actual words as "omnipotent," "infinitely powerful." He was now quite confident that he could make people do what he wished them to do (as he used to when he was a beautiful infant with red curls and an enchanting little face).

He decided he would not go abroad today, he would stay for the funeral, and when he did go away it would be on his honeymoon "with the girl of his dreams," i.e. Frances Smith. He was aware that she would have taken against him but he was now also quite sure that within a very short time of meeting her again, he would reverse the position.

It was not surprising because it is one of the interesting phenomena of life in a tower block, that the Indian girl's violent death was of interest to everyone on the north side of Fiery Beacon and to those on the south side, if they knew at all, it was of no more moment than if they had been living in the Antipodes. He barely remembered that these included his parents in their flat on the eighth floor, south side. He did not even wonder whether it would suddenly become clear to his parents that S. Ledge and W. Sledge were one person, their only child; they never did any thinking. When they remembered their son it was either to deny his existence or to grumble about his non-appearance; fault-finding was their only reaction to him, he thought viciously.

After Amrita's death, several people on the north side were kind, and would have continued to be kind but it was clear that their kindness was not wanted. It is possible that he could have made a number of friends; but it was unthinkable. He was on his own now, for a time, and when he was no longer on his own, he would be with Frances Smith. He was going on and up, without the help of neighbours or The Wotchas or anybody else.

On his own.

The Wotchas would have to dissolve quietly, as they would, without the leader; there need not be any ceremony or official farewell, the group must just fizzle out, and good luck to it. You had to be ruthless if you were going to get anywhere.

CHAPTER VIII

It was shortly after Sledge had left the Bogeys' flat on the day Amrita "fell" seventeen stories to her death that Mrs. Bogey arrived home unexpectedly; tired but smiling with pleasure that she had survived her air journey safely, even though it had meant a train from Manchester. Laden with presents from Ireland for her husband and son, she staggered out of the lift with her suitcase and entered her flat to find her son sitting on the hall floor with his head between his knees and a strange young lady in animated conversation with Mrs. Bogey's dear but helpless husband. After kissing her family she took off her hat and coat and hurried into the kitchen to make tea; there was a lot to be explained and tea was essential. It was the sort of situation in which she excelled.

There was an Irish tweed jacket for Joe and a toy leprechaun on a piece of elastic, which she pinned to the curtain in her husband's room "for luck"; Miss Frances Smith was accepted without question and tea dispensed. The first thing had to be an ecstatic description of the twins, which went on for several minutes. When the tea was drunk Mr. Bogey thought it was time for her to have a little rest but Mrs. Bogey swept all idea of "tiredness after her journey" aside. There was a crisis on and nothing, to Mrs. Bogey, was more stimulating.

She apologised for her delayed return; there had been trouble over the air ticket and she had had to wait at Dublin Airport until a cancelled seat on a plane had been available; she had had no opportunity to telephone. She looked from her husband to her son and across to Miss Frances Smith, half sitting on the window-sill, looking dreamily down to the bright, now shining river.

"Now what's been happening?" she wanted to know.

"It's Sledge!" Joe's Dad said.

83

Sledge's ugly visit, seen and heard by Frances Smith and certainly heard by his father, had somehow made Joe's troubles everybody's; his mother could not possibly have arrived home at a better moment. Joe Bogey's problem had become universal.

"It would be," Joe's Mum nodded, tapping her fingers restlessly, but that was the only way in which her manner fell short of perfection. She detested Sledge and suspected that he had led her son into situations which he would never otherwise have considered, but for the sake of keeping her small family together she had resolutely refrained from criticism. Nothing she heard about Sledge would surprise her; she only trusted vaguely in Joe's being "all right"; that belief only had kept her mouth shut over the years; that, and the hope that Joe would "grow out of Sledge."

But she was prepared for the worst and the worst it was: ". . . I've driven him often," Joe argued as though to himself, "you know that. Yes, I *do* know he often went on what you'd call 'robbery expeditions,' he always gave us an outline of what he was doing but we asked no questions. He went on a job, all I did was drive. Why did I? You might ask, Mum, but you haven't, so I'll tell you. (a) Because it was a bit of excitement, (b) Because I like driving (you paid for me to have lessons and I passed my test; what was I going to drive, eh?) And (c) biggest reason of all: I got paid well. Sometimes a fiver or it might be a tenner, and three or four times it's been twenty-five quid, just according. It's not gone on drink, girls or hashish," he said humbly, but hoping this might tell in his favour, "but gone into the bank, the one in King's Road near World's End."

The question of his own pizza bar did not for the moment arise; you can't start up a pizza bar from gaol and that was the only future Joe foresaw for himself now.

"Last night, no, the night before, was the same as had often happened before; he came for me at work. We went off, nothing special, the flat of an old lady in Kensington, silver whatnots, that was all. I wore the chauffeur's cap, like I've done often; drove him there; waited outside like it was for one of the people living in the flats . . . out he comes in his posh raincoat, the pockets swinging so I knew he was loaded, gets into the car and is sick all over his boots, so I know what . . ."

His mother nodded. "Of course," she agreed, "and so do I; he was always being sick when he went too far . . ."

"He'd gone too far all right. She was a Lady somebody, Bellhanger, that's it. He . . . he smothered her."

His mother nodded again: "I saw it in the evening papers; that was Sledge, was it?"

"And me," Joe said.

"You didn't move out of the car, son," Joe's father put in.

"Well, there it is . . ." Joe looked down at his hands, wondering what it would feel like to smother somebody.

"Except that he's been here just before you came home, Mum. My black pullover with the white phosphorescent initial on the back . . . I left it in Sledge's car . . . he planted it in the garden of the flats. It'll have been found by now."

They sat still, shocked into a tense silence.

"And where does *she* come in?" Joe's mother asked, looking at Frances Smith.

"I have just left home for good," Frances murmured quietly but she still could not resist putting it in the novelettish way she chose to think of it, "because my father was selling me to a business man, that's all."

"That's not all," Joe put in, "by a long chalk."

"It didn't take long for me to get into trouble, I must say," Frances agreed. "You may think I was looking for trouble and determined to get it. I suppose I was over-excited, which my nurse was always complaining about; 'she's over-excited,' Nanny used to say; it was supposed to explain everything. It may explain how I met your Sledge in a coffee bar and got talking, and how I let him carry my things to his car which was parked not far off, and how he took me to a kinky clothes shop and got me a job there, to start one day next week, I mean, and how I went off with him because it was a nice day and had tea at a hotel by the river in Maidenhead . . ."

"And how you didn't have a roll in the hay," Joe put in with scarlet face. "And how you've no intention of taking that kinky job."

"And how, when we got back to Chelsea, he was annoyed, I suppose, because I didn't want what Joe calls a roll in the hay, he pushed me out of the way, as I stood on the pavement, so that I couldn't reach for my things, slammed the door and drove off."

"He can't keep his fingers off of something for free," Joe grumbled.

"So I had nothing, not even my purse, and so, even though it was after closing time, all I could do was to go to the kinky clothes shop, luckily finding them still there, and ask them where he lived, and they told me here, and so I came."

"And all day she's been going from flat to flat, pretending to be a person employed in doing market research . . . looking for him."

"But I slept in your bed last night, Mrs. Bogey; you see, I went up to the roof to spend the night since I couldn't find Sledge, there wasn't anywhere else, and Joe came up by chance and met me there . . ."

"Found you, more like."

"Found, then."

"And now. Sledge looks like a madman; he's overexcited, if you like! He's just brought back her luggage . . ."

"I can't think why . . ."

Far from being crushed by this welter of complicated information Mrs. Bogey showed signs of being herself excited. "This is quite something to come back to, eh love?" She smiled at her husband. "It needs a bit of thinking out, planning, Joe lad; we might as well try to sleep on it tonight and *you* . . ." she looked thoughtfully at Frances, "can use Joe's bed and Joe can sleep on the sofa in the living-room and I'll have my own bed back, thanks; not that I'll sleep but I may as well be comfortable whilst I'm thinking things out. Now, Joe, get a move on, lad, you can't sit mooning about things; go and get yourself a couple of blankets from the airing cupboard; and *you*," again indicating Frances, "can take your things out of my room and tidy the bed. . . ."

Joe felt a warm comfort coming over him; he felt about eight years old and happy. His mother was behaving just as she used to, bossing, organising, coping with her unruly family; it made him happy because it was so different from her recent manner with him: looking past him, ignoring his remarks, turning her back to him and letting him hold forth, even leaving the room when he was in the middle of one of his diatribes against the older generation and their ways.

When they were alone together she turned to her prostrate husband whose great hollow eyes were, as always, watching her. She knelt down beside the bed and put her arms round him: "This is reel trouble, isn't it?"

"He'll have to go to the police soon," Joe's Dad said, "and that's for sure; it's the best thing, love."

"Not it," Mrs. Bogey said stoutly. "You leave it to me, love, I'll cope somehow; give me time to think, that's all I need."

About eleven-thirty, when the day-shift was starting work, Frances Smith went to the pizza bar and asked for Mr. Silas d'Ambrose. The young man who was working behind the counter had fair hair like a page boy of the Middle Ages and sulky features; Frances watched him, looking sulky to match, whilst Mrs. James Trelawny, a cigarette hanging from her lower lip, genteelly ran the mop between the spindly legs of the tables. "Waiting for Mr. d'Ambrose, are you?" Frances did not even bother to answer.

By the time Silas arrived there were half a dozen early customers enjoying their pizzas at three tables. He at once offered Frances a pizza which she accepted gratefully, but said that as she now had her handbag there was no need to treat her, she could pay for it, and did so.

"Do you mind taking me on behind the counter instead of Joe Bogey?" she said. "That's what I've come about."

Silas shook his head: "It's not a suitable job for a girl."

"Why not?" Frances asked in astonishment.

"Well ... for one thing ... it's heavy industry, turning that dough over."

"Women have turned dough over, kneaded it is the word, since Eve!"

"And then there's lifting that metal tray into the oven; it's heavy and it's got to be raised to shoulder-height!"

"Pooh! That's nothing."

"And you've got to be very nippy, quick, that it ..."

"I can be very quick when I want to."

"Why should you want to?"

"Because I can imagine things I might have to do which are much worse."

"Indeed?" A long pause, then: "No, I really do shun girls like you."

"Oh?"

"I see them sitting about in offices in their thousands, all looking bloody marvellous but doing damn' all; they only exist, it looks like, to take men's minds off the day's work. Oh no, thanks very much!"

"Look, you great big boob! I'm going to do this job; I've watched Joe and I know just how to do it; there's no ... no *mystique* about it; even you could do it, if you weren't so bloody lazy!"

Silas stared at her, frowning, raising his eyebrows, and frowning again.

"Yes, you're appallingly lazy; if I had a pizza bar I'd do the hard work myself and save the money paid to those kid-chefs!"

"Kid-chefs!" Silas repeated in great wonderment.

"Furthermore, I'd swab the floor myself and not leave it to Mrs. James Trelawny! All your profits are going on wages! All you do is to sit with your feet up, reading *Playboy* . . . that's what Joe said."

"That's not all I do," Silas scratched the back of his head wildly. "I take the cash and watch out that nobody escapes without paying."

She began to laugh, unaccountably; she laughed immoderately.

He started to laugh, too, until they both became slightly hysterical and Mrs. James Trelawny looked out from behind the curtain to the domestic quarters, in great disapproval.

"Great Scott!" Silas brought out a red spotted bandanna handkerchief, blew his nose and mopped his brow.

"That's a corny old one, my father uses that expression, Great Scott!"

"My father did too," Silas said, and they both started to laugh all over again.

"All right, you can have a go at it and you won't hold out more than one night, I'll bet. You can start tonight. Has Joe Bogey hopped it?"

She nodded. "When I got up this morning, he just wasn't there. His parents did not seem too worried, though. Mrs. Bogey suggested I come and ask you for his job till he turns up again."

Silas sobered up rapidly. "I thought that was about to happen."

"Explain."

"That Sledge friend of his; I've had my eye on that friend, or so-called friend, of Joe's for quite some time. It's only been a question of time; the Goody versus the Baddy, the Baddy always wins, doesn't he?"

"Why didn't you stop it, then?" Frances asked angrily.

"Because there wasn't the slightest chance of Joe taking any notice; surely you know that? What young chap ever listens to advice, especially such advice as: 'That friend of yours, Sledge, is no good to you, drop him.' "

"Well, this time it's . . ." she looked round and lowered her voice, "it's real trouble. Only murder!"

"An old woman in a Kensington flat or . . . ?"

"Um," she nodded again, "how did you guess?"

"It's his kind of thing, robbery with violence. That was yesterday's murder. Sledge called for Joe. I knew something was 'on.' Can't say I actually guessed but it is his kind of thing."

"Whose kind of thing?" she asked anxiously.

"That chap Sledge. He came the night before last to pick up Joe, just before closing-time; dressed up to kill . . . I mean that literally. Too confident, too, too confident. I thought it wouldn't be long . . . Personally, I'd have said he was a gun man."

"Not guns," she murmured sadly. "Hands, just his hands, Joe had nothing to do with it, he did not even go into the block of flats."

"I know, I know, he drove the Jag though. Oh, I know all about Joe's passion for driving. I suppose all these kids have to learn to drive and get a driving licence; and then the one thing they want to do is to drive. I know how much he enjoyed driving my MG, on the few occasions I have let him. This Sledge has a Jag . . . irresistible!"

"I wonder why Joe couldn't afford to buy himself a car, he gets paid here well enough."

"Don't you know? I thought you knew everything! He is saving up to buy his own business."

"Poor Joe," she said, her head drooping forward.

"Sledge has everything, things have come too, too easily to him; he is only, what, just over twenty-one? I've never known how old he is, probably younger; but he has a flat of his own and, believe it or not, he keeps an Indian mistress. What is there left for him? He is a young chap of unbounded energy and plenty of ideas and a perfectly appalling temper, he once had a fight in here with some chums with whom he lost his temper, laid about him like a mad thing. We had to call in the dicks to break it up. He is that type . . ."

"What type?"

"Started off being a criminal at a very early age; green lights all the way; what is there left? It's all come too easy."

"Do you think he murdered the old lady purposely, then?"

"I'm sure he didn't think he did; in fact, he would set out with the idea of not doing anyone any harm, but when he saw he was going to get caught with the loot, if he couldn't get out in time, say, or she caught him at it and tried to phone the police . . . well, he had to kill her; do you see?"

"Not quite, but you've done some thinking about it, I can see that."

"Three years running a place like this; you can't help but pick up lots of information about people, about the customers and what sort of guys they are; we've lots of regulars and some of them are the type of Sledge; we've often had the police along asking about someone or other they're after."

"Um."

"Now our Joe is a different type altogether; he is fundamentally secure; he enjoyed driving that Jag more than you or I could imagine; he possibly enjoyed getting the rake-off too; he wouldn't have liked the robbing though and he has some moral code, too."

"He's thoroughly scared now, anyway. I'm staying with the Bogeys; Mrs. Bogey came home from Ireland during the night; she's a marvellous person, and that poor husband of hers! I love them. They say I can stay in their flat. But when I got up this morning and I found Joe had hopped it—well, either he's gone to the police to Tell All, or he's just gone! It was his mother who suggested I come to you and ask if I can do Joe's job 'till he comes back,' she said. It could be that Joe has removed himself to save his parents in some way or other."

"My God!" Silas exclaimed, scribbling furiously on the table-top with a toothpick; "Oh, my sainted bloody Aunt!"

"Oh, my paws and whiskers!" Frances squeaked, "but *what*?"

"Aw hell!" Silas flung round from the tiny table and stared down at his feet. "If Sledge has had a taste of killing, he may do it again; it would be typical. It's the way a certain type of criminal behaves."

"You mean . . . he'll be out after Joe because Joe knows the lot?"

"Yes, I do; that would be the next move, Joe knows the lot, as you say . . . therefore it would be better from Sledge's point of view that he didn't live. I could be wrong, God help me, I hope I am."

Frances was appalled. "So the next thing will be Joe's body found somewhere around, on the waste ground where they park their cars at Fiery Beacon, for instance?"

"Oh, nothing as simple as that; it's much more difficult to convict if there is no body at all, isn't it?"

"I wouldn't know, but you're frightening me."

"I'm frightening myself. How can we possibly tranquillise ourselves by saying he has disappeared 'to save his parents'? It's not sense!"

"He was going to the police perhaps."

"That's just it. Did he get there, is what I want to know?"

"If he did he went at an extraordinary time, he was gone when I got up late this morning, and his Mum was bustling about, fully dressed, her face all closed up. Something happened between them, but she doesn't trust me enough to tell me." She looked across at Silas. "But who would blame her? I can't even trust myself!"

CHAPTER IX

It was, though, for S. Ledge as well as for W. Sledge, a harrowing time between the "accident" and the inquest; every time the door bell rang he had to go to the door and crouch down to peer out of the peephole to see who it was. He could, in his new role of killer-on-his-own, open the door to the police who came to make enquiries about his lost love but what about anyone calling on other matters, such as murder in Kensington? And one of the worrying things was the new look of the police in action.

Gone was the bumbling bobby; these new men were stern of purpose, without humour or the slightest possible joke; they had tight frozen faces and cold eyes.

In the absence of any suspicions (because how could they be suspicious of anyone as broken-up by the circumstances as S. Ledge?), they were scrupulously polite. Whilst they were there, civilly asking the obvious questions, S. Ledge could not take his eyes off the brown paper carrier into which he had neatly packed the gaudy finery he had so unwisely worn for his last job and carelessly not yet disposed of or even hidden. The orange polo-necked pullover was not fortunately showing over the top of the carrier at all, only the cream thick fisherman's knit showed slightly, very slightly, and there was nothing remarkable or unusual about it. Since they were there to investigate the apparent suicide of his best-beloved why should they evince any interest at all in the contents of a brown paper carrier with the names Marks and Spencer on the side?

Nor would they have if the times had not been out of joint.

They had come about the Indian girl.

The unexceptional questions went on: How long have you known her? Had she any family that you knew of? Where did you meet her? Had she ever threatened suicide? Has she been in hospital or shown any symptoms of mental illness?

He answered them all scrupulously. He answered all the questions as a law-abiding civilian, out of work owing to unfortunate strikes in the building trade, shocked and debilitated by the tragic event. They left in apparently subdued decency.

Though W. Sledge was as sharp as his schoolteachers had considered him, that word did not necessarily cover powers of observation; had it, he might have been even more jumpy than he was. Their civility as they left after the questioning lulled him into confidence, the hardness of their eyes meant nothing to him.

They were heavily silent in the police car, driving back to headquarters; they made their report for the inquest; it was only later when they were relaxing, their faces unfrozen, that one of them very simply said: "There's just one thing . . . why the dyed hair, um?"

The others nodded.

No one forgot.

It was Mrs. Bogey's ethos: "It's the small things that count, is what I always say . . ."

In ten years of occupation Fiery Beacon had harboured no more than the average amount of crime and only petty crime at that. Lower blocks were said to be cradles for criminals but Fiery Beacon had so far disproved that opinion. In the absence of garden fences over which to fraternise, lines of washing hanging out in tiny back gardens (none allowed at Fiery Beacon) and the fact that these inhabitants were Londoners and part of a terrifyingly big metropolis in which the next-door-neighbour played an almost non-existent part, Fiery Beacon did not house a community so much as a variety of workers and idlers. Upholstresses working at home, television writers, bank clerks, navvies, commercial artists, elderly retired couples, a Baptist minister, a poet who served in a grocery store, garage mechanics, salesmen, part-time hospital nurses; people whose lives and interests did not in any way impinge one upon the other.

The shocking death by a fall from the seventeenth floor only momentarily drew together those of the inhabitants of the north side who had been at home when it happened; but they were drawn by the passing tragedy and not by any mutual interest. Thus, what Mr. S. Ledge did with his life after the event was not really of interest, even to those who had shown signs of continuing to be friends.

No one either knew or cared whether or not he had acquired a new car, replacing the Jaguar. Here and there would be old ladies, peering out from behind their net curtains, but this activity is singularly uninteresting in a tower block, partly because amongst several hundred inhabitants one might never see the same person twice, or remember them if one did, and another reason was that above the first two or three floors it was only possible to see the ground immediately below by leaning out of the window, and then you saw only the top of people's heads as they went in and out. Even the make of car they possessed was unrecognisable from far above.

So when a young policewoman called at the neighbouring flat to that of S. Ledge she found it singularly unrewarding. This flat was on the same level as that of S. Ledge, the entrances from the same strip of balcony but divided by the lifts and two half floor-to-ceiling walls which effectively screened the doorways from each other. This neighbouring flat was occupied by two Italian waiters, long resident in England, so wrapped up in one another that they did not even know their neighbours by sight.

It was possible to live a more solitary and companionless life in Fiery Beacon than in the Western Desert; at least in the wild deserted places people greet one another in passing but not so in Fiery Beacon.

Thus, alone in his flat, S. Ledge mapped out his future for himself. He surveyed his financial affairs and affirmed that he had had one thousand eight hundred pounds in his current account at the bank; he had paid his rent for three months in advance, the electricity had been paid up to the last reading, he had bought a different car on part-exchange for cash and he had four hundred and thirty-six pounds and eleven pence left, taking into account what was under the floor boards.

He was in a much better position than any of the, as he thought, poor, pathetic train robbers, only one of whom at that time had not been captured and put into prison for thirty or so years. He had a lot more brain, he thought, for one thing; there had been too many involved in the train robbery whereas he, S. Ledge, worked on his own. The police had nothing against him, W. Sledge or S. Ledge, whereas all the world's police forces were out after the train robbers.

The bigger the amount of loot the bigger the organisation had to be, he realised, but on the other hand, how much safer to keep it small, even if the gains were proportionately less.

He was a tidy chap, that much he knew because it was the only fragment of praise for him that had come from his mother in years: "I will say this for Winston: he's a tidy boy."

His thoughts were tidy, too; look how wisely tidy it had been never to have given his receiver friend an inkling of where he lived! And keeping himself out of the way when Amrita received her male visitors had been another tidy move; keeping out of the way: those hours he had spent at the swimming baths, at the ice-skating rink in Bayswater, watching television in the big stores, going to race meetings, it had all been worthwhile.

Just one tiny slip annoyed him, that he had taken Frances Smith to find a job at the premises of people who knew him and knew where he lived. That certainly was irritating but he put his carelessness down to Love at First Sight. The subsequent snatching of her luggage had been a small mistake, too; intended as a tiny revenge, in a way, for her wordless rejection of him sex-wise.

But then ... if he had not taken her to "*I Was Napoleon's Mistress*" she would never have known his name or his address; she would have vanished out of his life since she never intended to take the job he so kindly found for her, and he would have been denied a fine future, married to a young lady of class and money.

Yes, Madame Joan's warnings had been timely, now he was taking care, it was, perhaps, a small pity that he did not go to the fortune-teller on the evening he went to collect Joe Bogey for their last "job." It was annoying that she kept such strict professional hours.

He had now killed two women, he said it aloud, sitting on the plastic-covered stool beside his spotless kitchen table. "I have killed two women." He said it again: "I have killed two women!" There was a kind of grandeur about it; he felt it to be satisfactory, somehow, that he should have killed two women, so neatly, so cleanly (well, perhaps not so cleanly in the case of Amrita) but cleanly in that there were no messy police court proceedings that led directly to him as the killer.

He knew it sounded crude and unkind but he could not help a slight feeling of pride in his work.

This being the day that poor little unfortunate Amrita was to be buried, three o'clock the time, Sledge knew the form, he had pride in a certain rectitude he found in himself, he dressed himself carefully in his neat tight black suit with the short sleeves and the newly bought black tie. It was seemly, he thought as he climbed into his car, that the upholstery was black; he would have preferred red but upon this occasion the sober black upholstery was just right. He drove to the undertakers. He had agreed to pay them thirty pounds in cash so he could hardly grumble at the attendance, which was four bearers, not their best by any means, merely their part-time ones, slightly down-at-heel and shiny-seated as to trousers. However, one could not have everything for thirty quid. Not even . . . not even a grave to oneself but a municipal multiple grave in a cheap part of the cemetery.

Having followed the hearse at a decent slow pace, in third gear, he parked the Rover beside the cemetery gates and followed the coffin being pushed on a trolley rather than carried shoulder-high, along the tarmac paths.

There was no parson and no prayers, by his own request. She was certainly not a Christian, with that red caste mark upon her forehead, and how could he possibly be expected to know whether she would like Buddhist or Moslem or Hindu prayers said over her remains? Rather than, as he put it, make a *faux pas* (he pronounced it foh par) he had requested nothing at all. After the coffin had been lowered into the clayey hole the bearers moved back and looked expectantly at W. Sledge, almost as though they were prepared for him to throw himself in, or was it merely that they expected a tip? He stepped forward and allowed to drop on to the lid of the poor quality wooden box a small, now rather faded bunch of violets which he had bought specially last night.

Wordlessly, disappointed perhaps, the undertakers withdrew, walking briskly back with the bier towards the main entrance, invisible from the graveside. A workman with a barrow passed and as Sledge stepper farther back from the graveside, trying not to soil his new shoes overmuch, he saw an Indian or Pakistani couple standing not far off, looking, surprisingly enough, at him. Though it was not a particularly cold day they were that curious colour, greyish green, which a member of that race can take on so pathetically. The woman was wearing a gaily coloured sari but over it a long tweed coat so that the only part of the sari that showed was mud-bespattered and dirty from the London streets. They looked dejected, cast out and brought into darkness; W. Sledge was not near enough to see that their eyes were of the chocolate-drop type; they only seemed to be peering out from deep, blue-grey caverns.

At him.

But what the hell?

He walked briskly and confidently away.

There were a few people about, some crouching over the graves of their loved ones, changing the water in the vases, laying flowers on the ground or taking away dead flowers. Sadly and ineffectually the foreign couple tagged along behind the living, and striding boldly, with his new self-confidence, W. Sledge. He now whistled as he walked, it was a relief to get poor Amrita decently buried, after the terrifying mess she had been in, it made him happy and light-hearted to have done the right thing by her poor broken body.

He swung through the gates and into the street, he fumbled in his pocket for the keys, fitting one into the lock, opened the door of his car. He sat for a few moments with the Rover fluff-fluffing luxuriously beside the pavement . . . no hurry because it contained a satisfied young man, a man, that is, completely satisfied with himself and all his works. A man, indeed, who found himself admirable in every possible way. And not only admirable but, to use his own words: Bloody marvellous! The foreign couple caught up by now and, standing at the gates, watched him drive away. What else was there to do?

And now . . . young Sledge he would a-wooing go, wearing the same clothes he had worn for the funeral, he took the brown paper carrier of clothes he had worn for the slaughter.

Sometimes, when he allowed his thoughts to go back to his unhappy encounter with Lady, Whatshername, Bellhanger, he had stabs of regret that he had been too cautious to take her gun and not leave it lying where it fell. Now, he very much wished he had, because guns could do a lot for you, with birds. He thought he could easily go to a gunsmith and buy one but he did not consider it wise. The trouble with guns, as he had so often told The Wotchas, was, they went off; occasionally when you didn't really mean them to. If he bought a gun from a gunsmith, the gunsmith would for sure inform the police (they did, he'd proved it) and if you didn't go for a licence they'd be after you. And if you *did*, well, they knew you were the owner of a gun.

At the time he had congratulated himself, as he so often did, on his foresight in not taking the gun which fell to the ground from the old lady's hand. If it ever came to a showdown, as it wouldn't of course, it would help to convince a possible jury that he had no intent to kill, but that *she* certainly had intent to kill, the murdering old so-and-so.

To get to the Bogeys' flat he had to go down to the ground floor and take the lift round the other side of the building, and this he did, carrying the brown paper carrier and whistling cheerfully and hopefully. He knew the form at the Bogeys' flat, you rang and waited to hear Pa Bogey's voice through the intercom beside the door.

"Who is it?"

"It's me, Mr. Bogey, Sledge."

"What do you want?"

"To see Joe."

"Joe's not at home."

"Can I see you then, Mr. Bogey, please?"

"But what about?"

"I owe Joe some money." That would do it, he thought, and it did.

To his surprise Mrs. Bogey opened the door, she was usually out at work at this time. "Come in," she said and, shutting the door after him, led him into the living-room where Mr. Bogey sat in front of the window in his chair, his lower limbs covered with a rug. Beside him was a chess board and Mr. Owland from downstairs was playing chess with him. This old man made no attempt to go when Sledge entered, the three adults stared at him with such intensity that Sledge began to wonder. He didn't have to wonder long. Mrs. Bogey had the whole thing worked out; he was now sure that Joe, as one might expect of such a contemptuous twit, having lost his nerve, had Told All. Sledge had always been slightly scared of Mrs. Bogey, she had brains, an accusation which could never be levelled at either of his own parents. Very often during the time he had known the family, Sledge had been brought up smartly by Mrs. Bogey but not so much of late, that is since Joe had been slowly fighting his way to freedom.

They did not ask him to sit down, they stared at him but not simply: in a frightening, complicated way.

He was just very slightly unnerved; he had meant to hold on to the brown paper carrier until such time as he had decided where to dispose of it but as it was, he was taken by surprise and put it down where he was standing, against a table leg; he brought out the bundle of notes for Joe, using both hands to count them, thus showing the others how much there was.

Wordless he handed it to Mrs. Bogey.

"Joe doesn't want it, thanks," Mrs. Bogey said quietly, "and he's finished with you, Sledge. He's grown up in these last few days."

"Oh he has, has he?" Sledge said nastily.

Mrs. Bogey gave her husband his cue by looking expectantly at him.

"Look, young man," Pa Bogey took over. "You're out, in this family anyway, I think you'll have a job explaining yourself to your Wotchas over this Bellhanger case. They don't want murder. Look, I'll bet none of them have been at your old meeting-place since it happened, am I right?"

Sledge didn't know because he hadn't been either; he hadn't seen any of them.

"Yes, they'll have hopped it at the sound of murder, like an ant-run vanishes when you spray it with insecticide, except for those who've fallen dead; they're left lying there . . . but in time even the ants venture out to remove the bodies."

Sledge took the tough line. "What the hell are you going on about?" he snarled. The cheek of it! Parents! Carrying on this way!

Mrs. Bogey took a soft line: "You see, we all know, everything. It's a pity for you because when a lot of people know a dead secret . . . it's dangerous, and you can't kill the lot of us."

Sledge received a small stab of fright; what did she mean by that? Could she possibly have been referring to the little domestic mishap of Amrita?

"Oh I see," he snapped back, "so you're keeping quiet to shield your tiny kid Joe, are you?"

"Not necessarily," Mrs. Bogey returned steadily. "If Joe's questioned, you're caught, that's for sure and *you know it.*"

"And if you're not caught," Mr. Bogey added, "you'll be on your own altogether in future and you'll be caught, sure as eggs is eggs."

Sledge couldn't help asking why.

"Why? Because you'll get more and more confident, of course; in fact I'd say you were that now, since you are quite sure you've got away with your girl-friend's suicide, aren't you?"

Sledge could have fainted, he could have swooned right away.

"You know," Mr. Bogey went on, "that disguise you're wearing, I was foxed for about five seconds after you came in, didn't recognise you, thought you were someone impersonating yourself, on the intercom."

Mrs. Bogey frowned slightly to warn him from going too far. Sledge had gone a more deathly white than usual; afterwards Mrs. Bogey confessed she had been "dead frightened, thought he was going to lay about and slay the lot of us."

But Sledge was far from slaughter just then, he was struggling with this awful weakness of his stomach nerves, he *had* to vomit.

He said something unintelligible and literally staggered from the room; still holding the money he had offered, he crossed the hall and slammed the door after him.

"What did he say?" Mr. Owland croaked.

"He said we'd all be sorry for this," Mrs. Bogey murmured absently; she stooped down and picked up the paper carrier, so carelessly left behind, pulling out the contents and spreading them on the table for the men to see. The jeans, the fisherman's knit sweater, the orange cotton pull-over with the polo neck, the beads . . .

She went over to Mr. Owland. "Well done, old sleuth!" she congratulated him. Mr. Owland chuckled, his head shaking from side to side. He was the only living soul on the south side who had paid attention to the tragic accident on the north side. Who had made a few discreet enquiries and put two and two together, that is, W. Sledge and S. Ledge. "Trust a chess-player," was the modest reply he had made to the praises of his friends, Mr. and Mrs. Bogey.

As often in the past, he was sick in the lift, going down to his parents' flat on the eighth floor. Still looking greenish and puffy, still carrying the fistful of money, he rang their bell. His mother was nearly always to be found at home in the daytime but he hadn't expected to see his father, who was having a day's rest. His mother cried out with surprise when she saw him.

"You're looking terrible!" she exclaimed. "Whatever have you done to yourself, Win?"

"He's dyed his hair," his father observed sourly; "To escape police detection, I suppose."

"Yer face is all sweaty, like when you're sick!" his mother screamed.

For a moment W. Sledge could not recollect why he had come. There was, in fact, no reason, it had been pure instinct, that of a sick animal returning to its pad, except that it was not the place he considered to be his pad. It betrayed a bad crack in his adult defences. He found himself holding the notes and thrust them forward.

"Here, you can have these."

"No ta!" his father barked shortly.

"What do you take us for?" his mother asked, looking greedily at the money. "You keep your hot cash to yourself."

"Bin turned out of your base in Colindale? Have you?" his father asked shrewdly. He knew this was no social call.

"Well, if it's shelter you've come for, Win, the answer is . . . no!"

"You chose to leave home, you've made your choice and that's it," his father added in agreement with his wife.

"And if the police come snooping round here I'll tell them straight," his mother's voice was rising, becoming more shrill.

"Tell them what?"

"Tell them you're dead rotten!"

"That's not evidence, that's opinion."

"Oh, you think you're so bloody clever . . ."

Ad nauseam.

There was naught for his comfort here. He left. When the front door slammed behind him, his parents were staring at the very slightly unrolling notes on the table in the manner of dogs put on *Trust* for a biscuit, watching the biscuit tensely until the words: *Paid for!*

Mr. Sledge wanted it for betting; Mrs. Sledge for Bingo.

It was a bad thing for someone whose nerves were already raw and stinging that he should arrive back at his flat on the seventeenth floor to find two dicks waiting for him. They seemed enormous, taking up so much room on the tiny sliver of a balcony outside the flat door. They were leaning over and staring down into the playground and rough ground where the cars were parked below, talking together as though they had all the time in eternity.

They turned slowly, greeting him in the manner they would use when expecting his arrival. "Mr. S, Sam would it be? Ledge?" Might they come in? They were not the ones he had met before.

His heart gave one of those curious bounds when he remembered where he had left the brown paper carrier. Fortunately his stomach was empty, he had only to make the effort to control the nervous retching.

Stopping a long way short of calling him Sir, they were civil, almost uninterested. It was a routine call, they said. It concerned a robbery and they were checking up on all the Jaguar cars in the district because one of these cars had been seen near where the robbery took place.

In the district ... that would mean on the outer edges of Chelsea and Battersea. In other words, the term was ambiguity itself, meaningless, he thought. And if they were referring to the Kensington robbery, where the old lady was murdered, why search for owners of Jaguar cars in Chelsea or Battersea, why not search the whole Metropolis, the whole of England, in fact; since, with the new motor-ways it was easy to go a long way in a short time now. Three hours after the robbery in Kensington the robbers in their Jaguar could be in Bristol, Birmingham, Leicester, Manchester almost.

"Come in and take a seat," S. Ledge said hospitably; he did not make the mistake of offering them a drink; it was not out of the wisdom but out of the repulsion from those four hard eyes.

In short: where had he been, could he very kindly give them an account of his movements a week ago tonight?

"What time?" S. Ledge snapped as though he had trumped a Jack.

But they knew all about that one and were not falling for it.

All evening, they replied. From, say, six to, say, eight o'clock the next morning.

S. Ledge said he was afraid that was going to be difficult; his beloved fiancée who would have been able to confirm what exactly happened that evening had taken her life the following day, and the shock of it had taken away his memory. Somehow or other he managed to make his eyes misty as he told them of the tragedy and they were suitably sympathetic. Still, they believed that if he really tried, he might be able to remember his movements immediately before the tragedy.

"Let's see now ..." S. Ledge certainly gave the appearance of trying very hard to remember and succeeded in squeezing out of himself the odd drops of information. He and his fiancée had had their tea, after which had gone out to a sexy film. Alone? Yes, alone, because she did not care for films and had had some sewing to do, she wore these lovely flimsy saris and they needed constant repair.

And what film?

He told them because that was actually what he had done, if not exactly at the time in question; he told them what it was about, at some length, enjoying the telling. He said he hadn't paid as much attention as he might because he had been thinking over turning in the Jaguar; there had been some engine trouble, again he went into details, and added that during his time in the cinema he had decided to change his car.

And after that?

After he came out of the cinema he went to the caff in Soho which he usually frequented; there he met some of his friends and talked over the trading-in of the car.

And then?

Towards midnight he had strolled along to meet another friend who worked in a pizza bar, whose work was over at midnight. He waited for him and had a pizza whilst waiting. He left with his friend and they took a taxi home.

Home?

Here, that is, Fiery Deacon.

And the friend?

"He lives here, in this block, round the other side, known him since we was kids."

And then?

Slightly surprised, S. Ledge raised his eyebrows: "To bed, of course."

One of them was making notes; after he had finished writing he waited, pen still poised, so evidently something more was expected.

S. Ledge then continued that he was by then so mad keen to get rid of the faulty car he had telephoned at an early hour to friends who ran an all-night garage in what he called Sarthend Road; they had told him they had a white Rover which had just been turned in, just the job. Naturally he was excited about this and started out early, so as not to be held up by the traffic. He was down there, well before eight, and stayed a couple of hours or more, they could check up if they liked, and he gave them the name and address of the garage.

"What a pity," he said at last, "what a pity my fiancée is not here to confirm everything you have heard!"

They asked him what his job was and he answered: "Labourer." He also mentioned the subcontractors for which firm he had, occasionally, worked; he went even further and mentioned the Barbican building site upon which he had worked for exactly one week, before they struck, or was it striked? His slight smile was lost on the po-faced ones.

There was a very long silence during which the writer wrote with, surely, exaggerated slowness. And S. Ledge thought hard as to whether he should make the kind of fuss an innocent one would make, wondering how it came that they were making such elaborate enquiries amongst Jag owners in reference to a simple robbery. Exclaiming at the badness of the times, asking if it was yet another bank robbery (surely not! Tch! Tch!).

Just as they were going the relief was so enormous that he unbent: "Don't you want the name of the pizza bar where my friend works? And what about my friend's name?"

But the casual, absentminded way in which they noted the answers to these questions showed him, without any doubt, that they already knew these answers.

In spite of his badly drooping spirits he managed to put on a hollow kind of jocular manner as they stood outside, waiting for the lift: "Well, I've told you the truth, and nothing but the truth," he joked. They received the pleasantry with the shadow of a smile, or even agreement; they nodded to him as they disappeared in the lift.

Disappointed at their lack of warmth, he stepped back to his flat. He had, in fact, deliberately not said "*the whole truth*"; but he sought to tell the truth because, as he always said, the best lies are the ones that are nearest the truth. The *truth minus* he called it; it didn't always work, of course.

CHAPTER X

It was all right, he told himself, as he dressed carefully in his courting kit, which he had not worn for months. It consisted of a pale apricot silk shirt, with a stand-up polo collar, the buttons being at the back, very, very smooth, and, in fact, not easy to do up, alone. Over this he wore a shiny black alpaca jacket which had but two buttons, fastening diagonally along one collar bone; it went on over the head. And as to trousers, he wore stretch pants in luminous acid yellow, so that in the pitch dark one could see these moving trousers: very giggle-making indeed, many girls had almost fainted with the shock and pleasure of it.

He looked at himself in the looking-glass with distaste; his black hair was a good disguise but did not go with the effective orange and lemon ensemble, which had been chosen to make the best of his flaming topknot. It was all right but the whole effect would not make people turn to look at him as they passed him in the street, which was just as well, perhaps. Under the circs.

Since it was quite clear that nothing was to be had out of the Bogey couple regarding Frances Smith, and incidentally about anything else, including their son Joe, he would have to find Joe and make sure that Frances was actually living in the Bogeys' flat and if this was so, W. Sledge was going to winkle her out somehow, if it meant watching the flat all day and night. He had now only one ambition left in the world and that was to "make" Frances Smith. Nothing but good could come of it. Since she was clearly a minor, there could be a reward put out by the rich parent for her return or for information. The parent might put an ad in one of the posh papers asking her to return and this Sledge would dutifully persuade her to do, himself taking her to her father's mansion as his bride. What could the old father do other than give his blessing to a young man who had so honourably . . . and so on. There were endless permutations and combinations in the Good Luck line, as fore-told by Madame Joan.

Now that he was going straight (and oh yes! he mustn't forget that!), now that he was going straight, everything must be straight in line with that; such as marriage in a register office and the lot.

It might not be long before he, too, had strings attached to his name, like that junky in "*I Was Napoleon's Mistress*" ... the Honourable. It sounded good and carried weight.

He would leave his car in the underground garage and take a taxi up West; even though Frances Smith "had it written all over her" this was going to be done the right way, with no fumbling business in the back of the new car.

He gave himself a final long look in the looking-glass which Amrita had had fixed to the back of the bathroom door. (Bless her, it was tactful of her not to be present this afternoon, when the dicks came!)

Considering how his nerves had played up today. all that sickness and that, it was marvellous how good he looked. He glanced round to make sure the flat was neat and tidy before he left and closed the front door after him. He flew down the concrete stairs in the old way, like he and Joe did when they were small boys. It made him feel good.

The day's shocks were not yet over, though, for what did he see when he went along a little before midnight, as he had so often done when Joe was on late shift? Above the crowd and the smoke, Miss Frances Smith, in a chef's hat and striped apron, serving pizzas.

She was extremely busy and did not appear to see him, but that stuck-up ass d'Ambrose saw him and strolled casually towards him. It was disappointing that his dyed hair was not more of a disguise but, of course, d'Ambrose may have been working his way across to him without recognising him, merely to greet another customer. W. Sledge did not wait to see, he slid out and sauntered casually up and down the pavement until he saw Frances Smith emerging from the pizza bar.

"Hallo!" he greeted her eagerly.

She simply hurried on; he had to run to keep up with her: "Don't you recognise me?" He caught hold of her shoulder and jerked her round to face him; she gave a sharp cry of surprise then looked at him contemptuously: "Had your hair dyed, I see!"

"I'm in mourning ... I want to apologise. I'm sorry I behaved so badly; it was a joke."

"What was?"

"Snatching your baggage like that."

"Very, very unfunny!"

"Go on, say you've forgiven me."

"But I haven't!"

"Don't you see? I did it for keeping in touch!"

"Don't be ridiculous, how could that 'keep in touch'?"

"Well, after all," he was aggrieved, "I did interdoos you to some of my friends ..."

"God!" she exclaimed, "I do believe you're half-witted. Leave me alone!"

"You've taken against me!"

"'Taken against you? I was never anything but, surely you can understand that. Do leave go of my shoulder please, or I'll start to scream."

Pavement squabbles are frequent on the stretch of Coventry Street upon which they were now standing; they were not even receiving curious glances. But he did let go of her and hurried along beside her as she went towards the tube station. "Where is Joe Bogey?"

"I've no idea!"

"Taken his job, then, have you?"

"Temporarily."

"Tell me, have the dicks bin after him with questions?"

"I've no idea."

"You can't kid me, I know you've got round Mrs. Bogey to let you stay, I know that. The Bogeys don't like me, never have; they think I've led their son astray. Poor me! Just because I'm the one with the ideers."

"Do go away," she begged, standing facing him now. "I don't like you, Sludge, or whatever your name is, I really *don't,* so eff off, do, and leave me alone."

"I'm going your way ... I live in Fiery Beacon too."

That was the trouble, she had not yet worked out the best way to get there from Piccadilly and wanted to ask a policeman, but she couldn't see one; the lone bobby soberly stepping it out along the pavement is as obsolete as a hansom cab.

"Let's get a taxi!" W. Sledge suggested brightly.

"Not on your life, boy!"

"You don't know the way, do you?" he said slyly. "You'll have to foller me, you're lost; don't know how to get to Battersea, might as well be Timbuctoo for all you know . . ."

She darted away from him with extreme speed and jumped into a vacant taxi which stopped so suddenly that the car behind it nearly ran into it and started blowing the horn irritably.

But he was after her as quickly and trying to wrench open the slammed door, with the other car behind now joining in the cacophony. Inside and holding the door handle, she screamed through the tiny driver's window: "Quick, quick, don't let him in and drive to Fiery Beacon."

She certainly fired the driver with enthusiasm but it did not matter how enthusiastic he was, with a solid block in front of him and an equally solid block behind, the lights ahead red, the pavements crowded, there was nothing he could do but look wild-eyed, clutch his steering wheel excitedly and rev up his engine.

A rowdy group of semi-drunken youths were bumping along the pavement, looking for trouble. They got the message upon the instant and with many cries of: "Aw, pack it up, leave the lady be, can't you see she's not playing?" they closed in upon Sledge and lifted him bodily, ridiculous trousers and all; laughing loudly and jeeringly, they deposited him with his back to the wall of Bob's Baked Potato Bar, where it had all started.

By now the lights had changed and the traffic moving off; Frances looked back through the dark glass of the rear window of her cab and saw him lolling against the wall, an absurdly dressed, white-faced golliwog, his hair having been severely milled in the scuffle he could do nothing more menacing to the jeering gang than shake his fist in weak rage.

Mrs. Bogey had said "Ask no questions" and because Frances loved them and wished to please them, she asked no questions, however agonisingly she wanted to know if they knew where Joe was. She let herself in with the key Mrs. Bogey had given her and heard Mrs. Bogey calling: "Is that you, dear? Come in."

She had put Mr. Bogey to bed and, in her dressing-gown, she was drinking some late-night beverage, and occasionally helping Mr. Bogey with his feeding cup. She looked extremely depressed but Mr. Bogey gave Frances a heartening wink.

"We've had the police, dear," Mrs. Bogey said soberly.

"But we was bound to," Pa Bogey said, "as I've bin telling the missis."

"They brought along a pullover Joe could have worn but, as I pointed out, there's hundreds of them around."

Mr. Bogey said comfortingly: "It was a routine call; we don't know much about each other in this paradise called Fiery Beacon but over the north side the inhabitants did know that amongst Winston's playmates was our Joe; their kid went to the same school after all, and not so long ago as all that. There's still the same headmaster at the school; he could have told them, if anybody else didn't, that Win and our Joe were buddies."

"They're getting very clever, are the police," Mrs. Bogey mused, "much cleverer than they used to be; and they don't make jokes any more."

"They've got to do a lot of asking," Mr. Bogey murmured, "we didn't ought to lose our nerves, bothering."

Frances, standing at the foot of the bed, said it was Sledge whom she found much more frightening than the police and told them about the scuffle she had had on the way home.

"If that happens to you again, scream," Mrs. Bogey advised. "There's nothing to equal a good real old tonsil-stretching scream. That and not going anywhere with him where there's no people around."

"Silas d'Ambrose warned me; 'Wait for me,' he said, 'don't go now, that rat-faced Sledge has just been in, with his shock of black hair.' He went smartly when he saw Silas had seen him. I couldn't wait for Silas, he was adding up."

"You watch out for Sledge, lassie," Mr. Bogey advised, "and as Mum says, scream." He made his strange choking sound, "My word, she couldn't half scream when she was a girl!"

Mrs. Bogey slapped him gently.

Frances looked thoughtfully from one to the other. How could they be so relaxed? Did they not realise how worried she was about Joe? Why were they not a great deal more so?

"Suppose I get into the lift and find Sledge is there?" Frances suggested with a shiver.

"I'll come down with you," Mrs. Bogey said comfortingly. "Not to worry, dear!"

"I seem to be out of the frying-pan, into the fire," Frances moaned, making a wry face. "Still, I'd rather have Sledge than, than someone else." Or would she?

"What was that, dear?"

"Oh, nothing," she said, turning away to go to the room allotted her. So they were not going to tell her, even if they knew, where Joe was; did they not trust her? But who could trust anybody? she wondered. She had known them a very short time; why should they trust her? Why, indeed, should anyone trust her when she couldn't even trust herself. Home and the wigged-one was better than this. After all, they couldn't carry her to the altar kicking and screaming. She could fight the wigged one tooth and nail so that the last thing in the world he would want would be to be married to the harridan.

Why had she not thought of that before?

Answer: because any excuse to get away from home was better than none; on her eighteenth birthday she had taken stock; where have I got myself? Nowhere but settling in as the daughter-at-home-looking-after father; and now she could see clearly why her father wanted her to marry the wigged-one in his mansion only a few acres away. Married, she could still look after her father, act as hostess when required.

She had longed to escape, to experience "adventure." Was this, then, the longed-for adventure? She thought: if it was, then for God's sake, acting hostess to a lot of boring old men talking about nothing but horses, who pinched your bottom the moment nobody was looking, was better . . . just. And as for "adventure," here she was, involved in, well, not actually involved in, but on the fringe of real crime, and what happened? This dear old couple were behaving as though they were at a Darby and Joan tea party; soothing words, smoothing-out, calming-down, brushing under the carpet! There is something nasty in the wood-shed, so don't look, will you?

It had all sounded so splendid, her father was *selling* her; poor little Frances Smith, she thought now, living in her gaudy, unreal, whodunnit world, quite alone.

Scream, Mrs. Bogey had advised. She felt like screaming all right; she flung herself upon Joe Bogey's ex-bed and screamed, but silently, into the pillow.

CHAPTER XI

Slipping was the only word he seemed able to formulate. Slipping! He ranged about the streets looking for an excuse to beat someone up. He passed the pizza bar, closed now. If he had half a brick he'd chuck it through the window. He looked up at the windows of Madame Joan's flat, blinds closely drawn; he could kick the door down.

He walked a mile and a bit back to the underground car-park; someone else was serving petrol tonight, they could always replace him! This character was a Pakistani who had rolled himself up comfortably against one of the pumps and was asleep.

He threaded his way between the cars in the damp and dripping cavern, found the Rover and drove through the park and out by the north gate and into the Edgware Road; he drove savagely, almost as though he were hoping for an accident; he drove out to the M1 and greatly relieved his feelings by standing on the accelerator, keeping it at a steady 90 mph. for nearly a hundred miles. When he shot off that highway into the comparatively country lane he slowed down, spent and flaccid. He looked for an all-night caff and found one.

Why did he bother with any of them, he asked himself, when he had wrapped himself round two plates of bangers and mash. Why bother? What on earth was it that held him to Fiery Beacon and the proximity of his parents? Why could he not just hop it for good and all, starting up afresh in, say, down-under? With his brains and his capital he could be living excellently and start again with a new name and a new habitat. Why bother?

The answer was that people were necessary for him; he had to show them. It wasn't the same, showing a lot of new people who didn't know him "from Adam"; it had to be the people who knew him, to make the impressing of them worth while. He tried telling himself that he never wanted to see that Frances Smith again, but it was only trying to kid himself. Though he hadn't known her above a week she was now the most important thing in his life. It wasn't that he was in love with her, or any of that kind of thing, it was just . . .

And where was Joe Bogey? Why did Joe have to branch out on his own and suddenly disappear just when it was important to have him near; was he simply scared stiff about being implicated in the Kensington robbery? And in hiding? Up to this he had never thought Joe a coward but now it seemed he was, after all. To simply opt out of everything at this stage was a disgusting, contemptible thing to do. Oh, it made him sick! If Joe was around he wouldn't half punish him!

However, Frances Smith was the most exciting, in fact the only exciting and interesting thing that had hit him for a very long time. Of course, he loathed the upper classes, that went without saying, but obviously they couldn't be done without; if there had been no upper classes how could he have made any capital at all? They certainly had their uses and he, Sledge, must keep that firmly in mind. This Frances Smith project of his was the only thing he had in mind at the moment and he decided that it must be worth following up. Its main attraction was that it made a change, therefore it was not boring yet. There were other, indefinable attractions . . .

There had been no trouble at all getting the girl talking on their first meeting; but she had clammed up rapidly; somewhere down by the river at Maidenhead, something had caused her to take against him; her manner had changed, she had become standoffish. As he had driven back he had burned with anger and that was why he had been so utterly stupid as to snatch her baggage. It wasn't greed or trying to be clever or anything like that; it was just that he was angry with her for not turning out the way he had hoped, that was it.

She had confided in him to begin with, up to a point. Where she had left off was over the practical details. It was all very well telling him she had run away from home because she didn't like her father or the man he had chosen for her to marry, but where did that get you? It may only have been that she enjoyed telling a colourful story. There had been details about her father and all that but she had been careful not to mention the name of the place or the name of the father.

There might be plenty of enjoyment to be had if he only knew these details. He could go on there now, for instance, arriving as the old gentleman was having his breakfast, with good news about his daughter; in his anxiety about her welfare the old chap would fork out some reward, that was for sure. Sledge felt a burst of warmth and friendliness for this old gent. He would, of course, for choice, not turn up in his snazzi-pants courting outfit, soiled after last night's manhandling, but who would take exception to luminous trousers when the welfare of a beautiful young daughter was at stake?

Thus a plan was formulated. Frances must be forced to tell him the necessary details, must be locked up until she did so, if she would not do so straightaway. If anyone interfered with the carrying out of this plan they would have to be wiped out, since it was so amazingly easy to get rid of nuisances, people who stuck their necks out or got in the way. Quite amazingly easy!

Sledge ambled back to London, thinking over his plans with enjoyment; he was so slow, in fact, that he was mixed up with the commuter traffic, the last thirty miles being solid with cars. He had breakfast and a fill up with petrol and oil in a motorway restaurant and on his way back into town, at one of those rows of shops along the suburban highway, he saw an ironmonger's; he went in and bought two stout bolts.

Back at Fiery Beacon, safe home, he was looking for a bradawl when the police came.

"Here again?" he said pleasantly as they showed him their search warrant. The fatheads! No, Sledge knew a lot more about search warrant activities than they did. Why did they bother? They never found anything of interest, that is, in the homes of anyone who was anything more than a half-wit! But they went on searching as a matter of convention. It pleased him that he should have left the flat so clean; he turned on the radio whilst they were at the job, cleaning his nails sedulously as he sat astride an arm of one of the overstuffed chairs in the living-room. They had a careful examination of the edges of the close-fitted carpets in every room, including (luxurious touch) the close-carpeted bathroom. It was insulting, really, the way they examined his clothes hanging in the fitted cupboard in the bedroom, but he supposed it had to be. Routine.

He tried not to think about the brown carrier-bag he had left with the Bogeys; it didn't do to get yourself scared at a time like this. They were thorough, though, they opened things like the tin of cocoa in the kitchen cupboard, knowing all about the cocoa-covered rolls of notes that could be found in such places. They took the dynamic pictures that he and Amrita had chosen together off the walls and examined the backs to see if they had been recently removed. They examined the bath panel, unscrewing the side and looking carefully under and behind the bath. In places that looked suspicious they ripped up the carpet; he was uneasy when they pulled out the bed, but of course he had been extremely careful about hammering those tacks home, and there wasn't a good light, either.

It was all done wordlessly; well, if they weren't going to talk, neither would he. He made himself comfortable, studying a motoring magazine. He knew a number of chaps who had had police searches in their flats or houses. It didn't mean much.

He couldn't make up his mind about the Bogeys, there were times when he knew they must go to the police with what information they had and there were other times, such as now, when he was quite certain they wouldn't; if he were implicated it followed that Joe would be; they were in this together, he often reminded himself; however casual Joe's involvement had been, they were in it together.

Joe and his pizza bar!

Apart from Joe, whose absence rankled more than somewhat, he felt pretty satisfied when the police had left. It was partly a matter of keeping your head; you couldn't help but win if you kept steady. Many people, for instance, would have been scared stiff by the police warrant, you had to keep steady; part of the object of the search was to make you lose your head, panic. He couldn't be nervous, he reminded himself, because he didn't feel in the least sick.

In the absence of anyone to talk to he decided to go to the receiver in Walham Green and try to find out how matters stood. What did he mean by "stood"? He did not know, nor would he ever have admitted to himself that he was uneasy; any excuse for talking, even to the receiver, was better than none. He brought out of his pocket the entrancing snuff-box or comfit box which he had stolen along with the other things from that wretched Mrs., sorry, Lady, Bellhanger. The tiger's tooth; he stared at it in the palm of his hand. He did not really want to part with it, he pressed it to his lips, kissing it: it would take the place of the caste-mark on Amrita's forehead which he used to kiss for luck: it was now his talisman. A strange, yellow, weirdly dirty object, it had immense appeal, redolent, as it was, of decadent Maharajahs, though perhaps not so decadent if the Maharajah happened to have killed its owner himself. The space for snuff at the root of the tooth was scarcely big enough for two of the smallest fingers, however, perhaps the Maharajah used it for tiny pep pills instead.

Mid-morning was not a good time to visit receivers unannounced; he might find him washing up for his wife, out shopping with a string bag or sitting in the local pub; though receivers are immensely powerful during the hours of darkness, in daylight they can be quite ordinary old gentlemen shuffling about their deadly respectable suburbs with nothing more in mind than they have in hand, their wives' shopping lists.

This particular one was doing his football pools at the kitchen table, no wife being present. W. Sledge tapped playfully upon the kitchen window and he looked up from his work, frowning when he saw who it was. He got up, however, and opened the back door. "What do you want?" he growled ungraciously.

W. Sledge assumed a look of one about to spring a delightful surprise, he edged himself past the portly figure of the receiver, into the warm kitchen, and, bringing the tiger's tooth out of his pocket he put it down on the kitchen table with appropriate ceremony. The receiver simply could not help himself, his hand shot out and he brought his magnifying lens out of the inside of his pullover, where it hung on a narrow cord, fitted it into his eye, and looked at the tiger's tooth closely. "How much?" he grunted at last.

"Two fifty," W. Sledge replied, adding, "to you!"

"Don't be ridicullus!" But it was an immensely saleable object and they both knew it.

"It's got everything," W. Sledge boasted, "luxury, violence . . ."

"Go on, say it, sex . . ."

"It wouldn't be in the window more than ten minutes in Old Bond Street!"

"But two fifty, you're joking!" The receiver made as though to return to his football pools. "You got no right to come without telephoning, you know it's against the rules . . ."

"But with a gem like this . . ."

"And there's other things is against the rules, if you don't mind me reminding you . . ." the receiver turned and gave him a long, indignant stare. "What about no violence, eh?"

"I don't know what you're going on about . . ." The tiger's tooth was now lying on the table. W. Sledge picked it up but held it delicately between his fingers, so that the receiver could still feast his eyes upon it.

"You do, all right, all right, that Lady Bellhanger . . ." the receiver evidently took sudden fright, remembering. "Go on, now, get out, will you? I don't have no truck with your kind, you know that."

"My kind!" W. Sledge exclaimed, astonished.

"Now look," the receiver said soberly, "I've always got the police comin' along: do I recognise this crest, have I ever seen that nutmeg grater or wine label? Sometimes I 'ave and sometimes I 'aven't. That's the way it works. I would hope it if I was you, you must be off your nut bringing me this thing, do you want to get yourself locked up? Or is it you've got to show off?"

"That doesn't mean a thing to me," W. Sledge boasted, "you've known me a long time and you know I never resorts to violence, never!"

"Excep' when you do."

"So you don't want this?" Sledge was gently tossing it in the palm of his hand.

"Not at your price, I don't!" But there was a recognisable note of regret in his voice.

"Okay, then, I'll be off."

"You do just that," the receiver advised. "And, in any case, just remember, I don't want to do no more business with you. I don't have nothing to do with robbery with violence, I've said that often enough; you should have got it into your head by now, whatever colour of hair you settle for!" But he couldn't resist adding: "A hundred quid for the old yellow tooth, and that's it."

W. Sledge made a hideous sound denoting sarcastic laughter. "Ta ra then!" He caused the Rover to put on a real spurt as he left Walham Green.

He had to wait some time to see Madame Joan and by the time she saw him her extra-sensory perception was full steam ahead, working to capacity. She refrained from comment on his black hair but she said at

YOUNG MAN, I THINK YOU'RE DYING

once that he had better take that nasty thing out of his pocket before she even started. Not in the least surprised, W. Sledge put the trophy down on the table in front of her.

"Not there!" she screamed, "over there on the window-sill, where we can't see it!"

Smiling knowingly W. Sledge did as he was told, then sat down and laid his hands out before her.

"What do you want me to tell you now?" she asked. "I've told you all I know."

"Tell me what to do next?" he begged.

"You can't expect me to advise you . . ." she said with distaste.

"What are you here for then?" he answered nastily.

Glaring at him she picked up his hands. She told him: "These are the worst hands I've seen for a very long time . . ." She would never overstep the bounds of her professional discretion and tell him exactly what she knew about his hands and, in fact, she was frightened of him; who knew but what he might strangle her if he took a dislike to her?

She assumed her professional manner saying that she observed he had been "crossed in love" since his last visit. "Things are not working out for you," she murmured, "I think, young man . . ."

"Yes?"

"Your future is . . ."

"Go on."

"Fluid . . ." She let go of his hands and waved her own vaguely in the air as though to demonstrate what she meant.

"How do you mean?"

She looked thoughtfully at him, choosing her words. "There's no future."

"What?"

"I mean, there's no future, that I can see, in what you're doing. What about a change of occupation?"

He smiled. "You're marvellous, ruddy marvellous. That's just what I'd hoped you'd say. You see, I'm thinking of changing my occupation . . . as you say."

"To what?" she asked, not caring in the least, in fact, thinking of something else but obliged to fill out the allotted time of the consultation.

"I thought that was where you might advise me; I'd like to do somethink abroad, I'm sick of this country; bad weather all the time, too many folk around, boring."

"Then go to Australia, dear, I should. Lovely warm weather all the time and no taxes to speak of; yes, that's where I would go, if I had no ties."

"That's it," he returned enthusiastically, "I thought you'd have something bright to say. Can you see me in Australia?"

"Oh yes, I *can*; that's where they used to send all our criminals . . . I mean, they don't now, of course; but what a delightful place to send a rotten bad man to, eh?" she laughed nervously, very much wishing he would go.

"That's it then," he decided, "I'll go round to the travel agency straight away."

"Emigration office would be best," she said, unobtrusively pressing the little bell fixed under her table top, a message to her "receptionist" to show the client out. As the remarkable-looking girl, her primrose hair piled up into a wobbly tower, showed him out he turned and waved his cheerful thanks to Madame Joan who muttered: "Except that he'll never get there!" but replied so that he could hear: "Anytime, anytime . . . ta ta!"

She knew perfectly well that he had left his bejewelled trinket on the window-sill but she ignored it as she went towards the kitchen, saying that she hoped her dinner was ready; she was "famished"; an onset of extra-sensory perception, such as she had had this morning, always left her extremely hungry.

W. Sledge felt hungry too and what better means could he have of satisfying it cheaply than going into the pizza bar downstairs? It was crowded but he found a table, and to his surprise he saw that Miss Frances Smith was on duty, the rota having evidently been changed, and that Silas d'Ambrose was lounging against the bar smoking a fancy cigarette, evidently making some entries into his account book. Mrs. James Trelawny put her head out from behind the curtain near which Sledge was sitting and he asked, "Has there been a change of rota?"

"Yes, Mr. d'Ambrose didn't think it suitable for the young lady to be on late shift, going home late at night, you know. Mr. d'Ambrose is making the pastry early himself—there's a surprise for you!"

W. Sledge nodded absently; he asked the man next to him to keep his place for him and sauntered between the tables to the bar.

Frances started visibly when she saw him but tried hard to appear unmoved by giving him the cold little smile she reserved for customers: "Which kind?"

Sledge pointed to the pizza of his choice, aware that Silas was now leaning against the bar, staring at him with his usual insolent stare. Neither of them said anything and Sledge picked up his plate of food, collected his implements in their paper napkin and went back to his table. He ate slowly, then went back to the counter for another. This time he could not catch Frances's eye. He ate the second one even more slowly; when he had finished it, nearly all the customers had left but Silas was still standing by the bar. Sledge waited, watching for a moment when his back was turned, attending to the changing of a five-pound note proffered by a customer. Then he leaned forward over the counter and hissed:

"Joe wants to see you!"

"Where is he?"

"I'll take you to him; it's secret; he's hiding."

"On the roof of Fiery Beacon?"

Sledge shook his head as Silas turned back towards them.

"Be seein' you," Sledge hissed, "outside Bob's, as soon as you're off."

Frances said: "He knows where Joe Bogey is, or seems to."

"You're not falling for that one, surely?" Silas remarked with some distaste.

"It could be true; what I don't understand is his parents taking it all so calmly; there must be a perfectly simple answer to it all, otherwise they'd be frantic. I've heard Mr. Bogey himself say that once there's enough people in a secret it's no longer a secret."

"So you'd risk going off somewhere with Desperado Sledge, to some hypothetical meeting-place where you'll see Joe again; all of you drawing rings round the police?"

Frances said: "You don't trust me, do you?"

"Not entirely."

"Well, perhaps you'll at least admit that I have a woman's instinct?"

"I certainly don't, whatever that may be."

"Well, I've got more common sense than you."

"You think so?"

Frances waved her hands wide apart: "The whole thing . . . it's out of hand; W. Sledge is ripe for anything now, he's got away with murder, after all."

"By no means, the police are well on his heels!"

"But they're so slow," she complained, "they let days slide by . . ."

"That's part of giving their suspect enough rope to hang himself, or rather part of getting enough evidence to secure an arrest; it's more important to arrest a man justly than to let a criminal go if there is any doubt as to his guilt."

"Ho ho! I don't think that at all, I'm like my square old Dad, a screaming fascist I suppose he's called. During the time they're collecting evidence against him, he could do an awful lot more damage and get himself out of the country. What is wanted is action *now* and I've got an idea."

"What sort of idea?"

"A pretty lethal one. Don't think I care a damn about W. Sledge one way or the other, but as long as he's swanning around there's going to be no peace and happiness for the Joe Bogey family and I adore them, they're sweeties, I even like Joe Bogey, *like* I said . . ."

Silas had vaulted the bar and picking her up, was swinging her round and round, whilst she kicked out her feet and Mrs. James Trelawny, having despatched her washers-up and on her way out herself, took one outraged look through the curtains and departed by the side door.

"I think I love you," Silas said, "God help me."

"I haven't time for that now," Frances replied briskly as she struggled free, untying her apron and tearing off her chef's hat.

"I'm taking you home . . ."

"You're not, you're not!"

"But don't you understand? I want to marry you. I must be mad!"

"Well, that would be nice but honestly . . . I've a lot on my mind at the moment. Thank you very much, Silas, all the same. The Bogeys have been so sweet to me, I've got to help them. Let's talk about it some other time . . ." and somehow or other she had slipped through his fingers and away.

"That's my girl!" W. Sledge snatched at her, hurrying tube-stationwards through the eternal crowd in Leicester Square. "The car is parked down there, just behind the Odeon . . ."

"Now look," she said, stopping suddenly. "I don't want any funny stuff; you said Joe Bogey wanted to see me, well, where is he?"

"In my flat, or will be by the time we get there, waiting outside, I should say."

"There's a big difference between waiting outside and being actually inside, because I'm not going into your flat and that's for sure."

He made fun of her, asking her if this was the girl who ran away from her wicked Daddy; he didn't believe a word of it. In the end she stepped quite meekly into the Rover, mistress of herself and of the situation, made over-confident perhaps by the very acceptable offer of marriage she had just received. She would really love to live with Silas, he was tall and thin and handsome and witty and not too young. She could really help him with his work and together they could open more and more pizza bars. Even her father could not complain that he was "not our class, dear," and would have no excuse for "cutting her off with a penny" with which he continually threatened her. It was a marvellous let-out and happening within a little over a week of her escape "from a fate worse than death" it was only just short of miraculous.

Sitting beside the young murderer she had a feeling of glorious elation, she was more than seeing life, she was taking part in it, she felt wildly happy, secure, wise and fulfilled.

She did not even wriggle away when Sledge put his arm across her shoulders as they walked from where he parked his car to the lift station at Fiery Beacon. "I love this block of flats," she said, "it's different, isn't it? There's something mysterious about it . . . all these people living so close to one another and yet not even knowing one another by sight. I wouldn't mind living here at all, right up at the top where the Bogeys live; it's out of this world, literally; you can hear the bells all over London and the fog horn, and the air is fresh . . ."

Arms folded, he was leaning against the side of the lift, gazing at her with a kind of fixed smile, not listening or hearing what she said, his mind on other things.

"But listen," she went on, "I don't know why I'm coming up in the lift this side because I'm not coming into your flat if Joe isn't there, truly I'm not, I mean it."

Even then she didn't have a trace of fear; she was as elated as though she were drunk, unimaginatively courageous.

They stepped out of the lift and a few paces to the left, past the half wall which protruded outwards, screening one entrance from the other. There was no one outside Sledge's flat; but the fascination of looking over drew Frances to the balcony edge and she laid her arms along the rail and stared out at the view, steaming London with the muffled sound of traffic.

Relaxed, W. Sledge once again threw his arm across her shoulders, ignoring the violent start she now gave at his touch. "Do you know what I'm planning to do? Emigrate, only I've enough money to do it quick, not Government sponsored."

"Oh, where to?"

"I was thinking about Australia, it's marvellous there. I've been taking advice about it."

"Who from?"

"Well, for one thing I've bin along to a travel bureau, like. I've heard about how it's cold down in the south and warm in the north and you've got this marvellous sea and loverly sands, not crowded. And loverly freedom."

"Freedom?"

"Well, you know what I mean. Free and easy, not with the police always poking around, everybody suspicious of you . . . like here. I could take this new car and . . . come with me, Frances, we'd make it together marvellous!"

"I can't do that, all the same."

"You'd like it with me. I'm a marvellous nice guy, really I am . . ."

"Sorry but I'm fixed up."

"Not Joe Bogey!" he exclaimed, aghast.

"No," she snapped, "a grown-up, a real grown-up man."

"Well, well, that's quick work," he said nastily. After a very long pause, during which she stared dreamily out into space he said: "There's a fortune teller I know says I'm going there for sure, and you're in it too."

"Well, she's wrong."

"She can't be wrong, she sees what she sees. Why not come along to her with me, ter-morrer, maybe, and you'll hear what she has to say."

"Not on your life, boy!" a favourite phrase with her, evidently.

"Aw, cummon, Frances, don't be like that. She's only above the pizza bar, Madame Joan. Marvellous! Oh, Christ!" he started patting himself, his pockets, his hip pocket. "Aw hell!"

"What's wrong now?"

"My tiger's tooth! I've blooming well left it there, I was so excited. Well, that's a bit of bad luck! I reckon I'm slippin'; I'm leaving things all over the place, absent-minded, that's what; I need a rest . . ."

"Well, never mind about that now, where is Joe Bogey?"

He glanced at his wristwatch: "Should be here any time now. Come in and get us a cuppa, eh?"

"I said no and I meant no!"

He turned away and, taking out his keys, unlocked the door at both locks and went into the flat. She heard him fill the kettle and bang it on to the stove, she heard the electric switch being turned. He came out again.

"Come in, Frances, come in, don't, *don't* be like that."

"It's not a question of 'being like that,' I'm just not coming in and that's that."

"Well, I'll have to bring you out a cuppa."

"No you won't, I came to see Joe Bogey and as he's not here, I'm off."

"Give us a chance," he begged. "Joe's hiding, keeping out of the way of the police because he's dead scared about that little adventure we had a week ago."

"Hiding isn't doing himself any good, it's admitting guilt."

"Of course, but that's what I'm hoping you'll tell him! I've got confidence; I know the police have to have enough evidence before they start arresting, and I know about how much evidence they have and it's not a lot. Old Joe loses his nerve too easy, that's what!"

Frances continued to lean against the rail, her feet crossed one over the other, her back to the front door of the flat and to W. Sledge. She could not, therefore, see his face.

The lid of the kettle started to blup-blup up and down, the water inside now boiling, but W. Sledge stood in his doorway and looked at Frances with her back turned to him, with what he was about to do written all over his face. What a kid she was!

"There goes the kettle!" he exclaimed, his voice slightly strangled from excitement. He moved the doormat with his foot, without looking down at what he was doing, he was wedging the door open. He said: "Well, I'll have to go and make the tea, if you won't ..." and as he uttered the words he stepped forward and with a single movement put his hand, holding a tea towel over Frances's mouth, pressing her head back as he had pressed the head of the widow in Kensington, putting a vice-like grip round her tiny waist with the other arm and pulling her back into the flat, across the hall, where her wildly flailing legs kicked over the telephone table and displaced the few mats strewn over the fitted carpet, and through the open door of the tiny bathroom. He thrust her inside so violently that she fell face downwards on the fitted carpet; he slammed the door, bolting the two newly fixed bolts, top and bottom.

Then he went into the kitchen and made himself a pot of tea. "Serve her right for being so bloody stupid, if she wasn't frightened of me she bloody well ought to have been, silly, sloppy, stupid kid!"

CHAPTER XII

"It's like this, Mr. Bogey," the kind policeman was saying, "so long as we don't know where your son is, he's by way of being a suspect in the affair of the Bellhanger lady. I personally don't for one moment believe your son is a killer; from what we have heard about him from his late headmaster, that's not your Joe's line. But he was always very easily influenced, and I confirmed this with another teacher, who possibly knew him better."

"I'm afraid you're right there, Officer," Mr. Bogey agreed sadly. "There was a time when I was his hero, so I should know; there was nothing I couldn't do with that little lad, if I'd wanted. He was ready for any game I suggested, not necessarily adventure but anything with a bit of glamour to it; these old-fashioned adventure stories, like *King Solomon's Mines* and all that; you could set him alight with a bit of reading to him; it wasn't half fun, playing with him, like."

"Well, you do see my difficulty, Mr. Bogey. It's hard to have to say it, but so long as he's not around, he's suspect."

"That's all very well, Officer," Mr. Bogey argued with deep respect, "but if he was 'around' as you call it, he'd be suspect too, since you've got what *might* be his pullover in your possession, found on 'the site,' as it were ..."

"Mr. Bogey ... are you sure you can give me no clue as to the present whereabouts of your son, Joe?" The policeman's attitude had stiffened, there was no doubt about that.

"I swear to you, Officer, that at this moment I do not know exactly where my son Joe is."

"'Exactly,'" the policeman repeated, chewing over the word. "'Exactly.'" He stood staring down at the cripple, who returned his look with a wide open, frank stare.

"Why pick on *me?*" Mr. Bogey asked pathetically. "What possible use could I be to an ..." he hesitated over the word but brought it out triumphantly, "an absconding son? Have you a son yourself, may I ask, Officer?"

Alas, the policeman had two.

"Well then? Just how much do you think you know about their activities?"

It was unanswerable. Check and mate, as Mr. Owland from downstairs would say.

"Let us know if you have any news at all, won't you?" Mrs. Bogey begged as she let the officer and his silent assistant out of her flat.

"Isn't it funny," the Inspector remarked as they went down in the lift, "how you'll take anything from a physical wreck like him? He exudes a kind of goodness that you can't doubt."

"Can't you?" the silent one put in finally, "I can."

"You think he was lying?"

"Indeed I don't. He was being quite, quite candid, as befitting a pathetic and clearly good-through-and-through cripple."

"What the dickens do you mean?"

"It's the word *exactly*; he meant what he said and it was the sober truth, he doesn't know *exactly* where his son is. Do you ever, at any moment, know *exactly* where your sons are?"

But they did not leave Fiery Beacon; they walked round to the north side and took the lift up to the seventeenth floor, stepping out on to the balcony just as W. Sledge was stooping down to pull the doormat out of the way, so that he could close the door. He started so violently that his start could have been seen several yards away. It was the two policemen who had been before, eyes frozen over as they said, "Winston Sledge, isn't it? Or Sam, er, Ledge?"

"Coo, Officer, you gave me a fright; just doing a spot of housework!" He gave a nervous laugh but was now apparently more than relaxed. "Come in, do!" So this was it, she would scream and it would be all over; why didn't she scream and "let's have done with it all," he thought, wondering how long it would be before he retched and was sick like a dog on the doormat in front of him.

But now they wanted to ask about Joe Bogey and also to see how he reacted to their use of both his Sledge-like names; it seemed ridiculous that two such large men should wish to squeeze into such a small flat and sit down for the short time they stayed. It was as though they wished to familiarise themselves with their surroundings. They, in fact, stared round.

Scream, damn you, scream! Thump on the door! Scream the place down and then it will be all over! No more worries; just a lifer, and time for "me nerves" to settle down. The formality, the extreme courtesy, the glazed eyes: Christ, it was getting him down! He was going to be sick, he knew he was. "Just a minute!" he rushed from the room and leaned over the kitchen sink, heaving. No vomit came, he turned on the tap and dabbed his forehead with cold water, drying it with a tea towel.

He was back in less than a minute in the living-room. There they sat, as though there for life, paying a courtesy call. They turned their blank faces to him, but observing his sweaty white face, his black, black hair . . .

"So you have no idea where your friend Joe Bogey is, none at all?"

Beyond words, W. Sledge, sick, shook his head. They were actually going. They went. Without a word to one another they descended in the lift, they walked across the parking lot to the waiting car. They got in.

"He's dead; he'd have to be; he is the only person who can give evidence over the Kensington-Bellhanger thing; so he'd have to be killed. It's only a question of when the body will turn up."

The other wriggled uncomfortably. "No, I can't agree there, I'm not sure. That smooth-faced cripple and his attractive little wife, they were altogether too, too relaxed!"

"Like to take a bet on it?"

"Not more than ten bob."

"Taken."

He couldn't stand it any longer, he banged on the door.

Silence.

He kicked the door, he got angry and kicked wildly, as though he were trying to break it down. "Damn you! Damn you! Damn you!" he screamed; he beat his fists against it, he kicked again and again.

He sat down on the telephone chair, head in his hands, and cried. He couldn't be sick so he cried. What was the matter with the damn' girl, keeping dead quiet like that? Had he killed her?

That was it, he'd killed her. Killing was altogether too, too easy. He'd done it once, he meant twice . . . it was nothing, no force, nothing. They were there and alive and suddenly they were not there, they were dead.

And it wasn't as though he'd wanted to kill either of them, any of them. It was not what he had intended, this last thing, not at all what he had had in mind.

It was more ... something like that marvellous film he had seen, a chap gets this girl as a prisoner in the cellar of his house, keeps her there for weeks, months, gets to know her. It wasn't sex he wanted so much as ... well, what was it? Having this hold over her, knowing that her life was in his hands, he could kill her or rape her or do anything else with her, she was his, quite, quite his. That was the sort of thing he'd had in mind, keeping her, looking after her and torturing her if necessary until she agreed to do what he wanted, which was to go off to Australia with him and the Rover.

He'd had this locking-up lark in mind over Amrita, after he had seen that film; he'd actually said to her that he'd a damn' good mind to shut her up, like that, in the bathroom and she'd laughed and asked why. And he couldn't say why. Only he did point out how excellent a place the bathroom would be, since, from top to bottom of the flats, the bathrooms, built one over the other, were part of the lift shaft, central to the building, the pipes and electric cables and air shafts all going up the centre shaft. There was ventilation but no windows in the bathrooms, and you could hammer your way right through the walls to find yourself in the vast dark nowhere; you could scream yourself silly, locked inside one of these continental-type bathrooms, no one could possibly hear you.

He'd done it now, though; what was wrong with her, he wondered? It must be she'd dropped dead from the shock and that was that. And he didn't feel inclined to open the bathroom door to find out, in fact, he knew for sure he was never going to open that door; the last corpse he had seen, only the other day, had been too utterly terrible; he was not going to look at any more dead people, thanks.

He gave her one more chance, kicking and shouting and banging on the bathroom door; no answer. Nothing. Nix.

So now he would have to be off, get out of the country as quickly as possible. *Drive* to Australia, that was what. *Drive* there!

He could start as soon as he had collected his money from the bank.

He glanced at his wristwatch, too late now, but there was still time to go and get his talisman from Madame Joan. He went to the bathroom door, just once again, and kicked it. "I'm off to Australia!" he shouted, "so do you hear that, you bloody bitch?"

Dead silence, of course. God! how easily people died; how miserably fragile was an old woman's neck, a girl's neck, any neck, it seemed. And that girl had such a damned long neck, it was one of the things that had attracted him. So long that it broke too easy, that was it. He'd broken her neck—clickety-click!

"Bye-bye, then!" he screamed and slammed the door after him as he went out.

The afternoon had fled past, it was five minutes to five when he rang Madame Joan's bell; the blonde with the pyramid hair opened the door to him: "Yes?"

"Could Madame Joan see me for a minute?"

"Have you an appointment?"

Of course he hadn't, any fool could see that. He only wanted his tiger's tooth back.

"No, I saw her this morning, I left something. I've called for it."

"What was it?"

"A little . . ." he couldn't think of a sensible name for it, he felt a fool saying he'd called for his tiger's tooth. "A trinket," he gobbled, "a small thing which I value for sentimental reasons."

"I'll go and see."

"Thanks." He didn't get asked in so he had to stand in the open doorway, on first one leg, then the other.

She returned: "Madame says what kind of small thing?"

He frowned deeply and darkly; so she was going to be like that, was she? "A bloody tiger's tooth," he returned angrily, "Indian, silver-mounted."

She went away and returned quickly.

"Madame says she hasn't seen a tiger's tooth, and she's with a client now, I didn't ought to disturb her . . ."

"You'll go and bloody well disturb her again and ask her to give me back my tiger's tooth!"

The fantastic creature rolled her eyes, asking her Maker for help and protection from this impossible creature. Madame herself came to the door this time, her face a mask of non-comprehension. "Young man," she asked sternly, "what is the matter with you? Are you ill?"

Apologetically, he explained. She was probably the only person who had ever made him feel apologetic, almost humble.

She drew herself up with great dignity. "Young man, if I had found your ... your whatever it is you have left, I would, of course, return it to you, as I have found nothing, I cannot return anything. Be reasonable, please!"

"On the window-sill ..."

"You have left it somewhere else, not here!"

And because she was no ordinary person but an oracle he accepted her behaviour meekly, thanking her and turning away. She shut the door, very gently, and took the tiger's tooth out of her pocket, holding it in the palm of her hand and looking down at it, sadly perhaps. She slipped it back into her pocket, still holding it in her hand.

The receptionist was standing at the top of the stairs, looking quite put out.

"Don't worry," she said gently.

"I'm frightened of him," the girl whimpered. "What shall I do if he comes again?"

"He won't."

"He will, I'm sure he will!"

Madame Joan shook her head. "He won't, you know." She walked upstairs towards her front parlour or consulting room where the client was patiently awaiting the resumption of her interrupted session.

She clutched the attractive object in her pocket; to have returned it to the young man would have been wasteful, as wilfully extravagant as throwing it out of a moving railway carriage window.

"He will not be back, you will see; it would have been extremely foolish of me to return his little toy, because he's dying."

The receptionist stood aside to let her pass. "One sunset from now, perhaps, two sunsets at the most ... he will be dead."

And because she never forgot the libation she felt she should always make to the gods, she added, like touching wood: "I think ..."

She sat with her back against the bath, arms round her knees, chin on knees, starry-eyed at her own cleverness. A cleverness, of course, stemming from absolute confidence because her lover-boy Silas d'Ambrose would be cantering to her rescue, if not exactly upon a white charger, at least in his red MG. So if she kept absolutely quiet she would, between now and her rescue, reduce to a gibbering lunatic W. Sledge.

The self-congratulation was so glowing and fulsome that for well over an hour it blinded her to the stark but bitter little truth. *She* knew that W. Sledge had bifurcated and was also someone with a flat in the same block as his Mum and Dad, because he had told her so, in the first fine careless rapture of their acquaintanceship, before everything was spoiled by his clumsy and greedy bag-snatching. But now she could not remember discussing this detail with anybody; it happened, as it seemed, so long ago, so very much had taken place since, in short, she had forgotten it. Did Silas know? Did the Bogeys know? Did the police know?

At first there seemed to be a lot going on, people arriving, voices, people leaving. Then W. Sledge's attack on the door, his evident hysteria and his departure, slamming the front door noisily. Australia? Ha ha! As if she would believe that! Then silence, and it was only after rather a lot of this absolutely dead silence that the questions came to her.

Within seconds she was drenched with sweat, the hair at the back of her neck wet and pricking, her pride in her own cleverness a punctured balloon. Perhaps he had it in mind to do a "collector" on her: the collector in the film was a schizophrenic who collected young girls, kept them locked up, as any collector keeps his treasure locked up.

She picked up a tin of bath cleaner and banged it against all four walls in turn; it made surprisingly little sound and had no effect whatever. To calm herself she turned on the bath water, undressed and had a bath. She felt better afterwards, fluffing out her short hair with her fingers and peering anxiously at herself in the looking-glass above the basin.

Then she heard him come in. She heard him come close to the bathroom door, so close he was almost breathing down the crack.

She shouted: "Well, have you finished your silly joke? I suppose you think you're *The Collector,* do you? Well, it's a flop!"

He clung to the door, gasping with relief. He had had to come back, there was nowhere else to go. He had wanted to make enquiries as to bookings on cross-channel car ferries, but there had been no time after he had been to pick up his tiger's tooth from Madame Joan, everywhere was closing, it was five-thirty. Much as he did not want to, he had to go back to his pad and he intended to pack everything he wished to take and leave the place, never to return.

But how marvellously quickly, minute to minute, his prospects changed! He knew that it was an immense relief to discover that she was not dead but his adjustment to the fact of her death had been complete for the past two hours and it was not only a shock but an annoyance to have to reverse everything yet again.

"Open the door please," she begged. "I've been in here long enough."

He stood there, leaning against the door jamb, still slightly breathless from shock; he didn't answer because he couldn't. His mind crawled back to all the fine rolling phrases which he had turned over in his mind again and again; he was going to wear her down, intimidate her, tame and train her to obey, and a whole lot of other jabberwocky which he couldn't for the life of him remember now; stern, powerful, W. Sledge-type things. And all he could do now was to gasp with relief.

He did not formulate the words, but he was grasping the misty idea that to keep up young-thuggery it was necessary to maintain one's aims and ambitions, not to mess about and change, dither around. It was that Lady Bellhanger that had started it, with the gun and the open mouth. If he hadn't had to deal with those two menaces he would never have lost his nerve like this. It wasn't fair to have brought the gun into it; after all, *he* didn't carry a gun. It was shocking to suddenly find yourself looking straight at the barrel of a gun, held by a dear old lady like that! It had been the root and cause of all his troubles, it had broken his nerve, caused him to lose confidence and to give way to his sickening weakness, his nerves.

She put her mouth close to the door: "Are you there, Sledgey? Open the door, there's a dear, you've had your joke. You've won!"

He didn't give way at once but a corpse in the bathroom and a quiet clearing out to the other side of the world was one thing and a real live girl, bolted into the bathroom whilst he made his getaway, was another. Of course, he could slip off and leave her to starve to death; the rent was paid for three months ahead, no one could want to get in and there was no reason for anyone to break down the doors, unless they suspected she was there, and how could they? The police had had their routine search, they would hardly need another so soon, or indeed, ever again.

But then, he liked her, so why should he think up such a cruel fate for her? She had never, in fact, done him any harm, or not much, so why should he leave her to a cruel, slow, slow starving to death?

He unbolted the top bolt he had so carefully fixed into place and after a long pause for decision he shot back the bottom one. He went into the living-room and lay down on the sofa, lighting a cigarette and looking at his feet resting on the arm of the sofa. He waited for her to come out and he did not even turn his head when she came into the room.

"We could start again," she said briskly, because she had made up her mind, "from where we left off."

"In what way?"

"When I first met you in the coffee bar; I liked you, that's why I went in your Jag to Maidenhead. Since you snatched my baggage in that stupid way and then brought it back, in an even more stupid way, our friendship hasn't progressed at all."

"'Hasn't progressed at all,'" he mimicked, he loved the way she spoke.

"So what have you got on your mind for us now?"

"Will you come to Australia with me?"

"Yes," she said boldly, falsely disarming. It was almost shocking, like stepping off a bottom stair that wasn't there.

"Why?"

She shrugged.

"But why?"

"We might make a go of it!"

"I've looked at the map, we can travel nearly all the way overland, through Persia and Afghanistan, I know people who've been that way, hitch-hiking; none of them, that I know of, got themselves to Australia, they got taken up with India on the way."

"Have you a passport?"

"Yep, have you?"

She nodded.

He stretched out his arms: "Come and kiss me then."

"Oh no, not that!"

He scowled.

"I . . ." she paused, choosing her words, "I don't feel that way towards you, honestly. But why worry? You'd have to grow out that ghastly black hair, to please me physically."

"What if I did that?"

Again she shrugged.

"Now look, let's get things straight. I can shove you in there again and bolt the door and pack up my things and go, and then where would you be?"

She shuddered involuntarily but, still bold, returned cheekily: "In there!"

"So I mean business. If you're coming you'll have to go to the Bogeys' flat and get your traps and you have to do it on the understanding that I'll kill you if you so much as open your mouth. I'll watch the Bogeys' flat until she's gone out and then you'll go . . . have they given you a key?"

They had.

"Then you'll go in and get your things and if Mr. Bogey shouts, you won't reply because if you do . . . well, you'll know what will happen to you, *and* I mean it." Then, after a pause, he said casually: "And where is Joe?"

"Yes, where?"

"You don't know?"

"I've no idea. I didn't want to ask the Bogeys, I felt they didn't want me to, I should say. So there's a snag to your plan; you may watch the flat and see Mrs. Bogey depart to work but what if Joe is back, or has been coming back home for food . . . or something?"

Yes, indeed, what then?

Neither of them spoke, he pressed out the cigarette stub and folded his arms.

She went very white, her lips were stiff, but she managed to control her voice when she said: "So you *have* killed Joe Bogey!"

No answer.

"That's what everyone was frightened of; the Bogeys didn't even mention his name, they're too . . . oh, I don't know."

"Well," W. Sledge gesticulated vaguely, "it was obvious, wasn't it? It was either him or me!"

She gasped.

"He knew what happened that night in Kensington, it was only a matter of time before he came out with it, his parents would of made him go to the police because the police are after him, since they found his pullover on the spot. There's more evidence over that Bellhanger thing against *him* than there is against *me*."

"God!"

"As it happens, I'm getting careless, I'm slipping, and that's why I'm getting out. It's me nerves. I've had enough of it. I left my clothes what I wore that night in a carrier in the Bogeys' flat; I didn't mean to, of course, I was on my way out with them, down to the river, going to weight them down with bricks till they sank good and proper. So ... that puts the Bogeys right in it, up to the back teeth, don't it? I don't wish old Pa Bogey any ill-will, he's got enough to put up with. Much the best thing to do was remove Joe from trouble; his parents will never know, they'll spend their lives thinking he'll turn up, they won't dare to go to the police with the carrier of clothes and ... well, that's it, isn't it!"

"My God!"

She sat down in a low chair, clasping her arms round her knees and rocking herself slightly. Then she suddenly burst out crying, not sad slow tears but hysterical loud sobs, she got up and started to batter W. Sledge with her fists; he threw her off, resuming his nonchalant pose and she lay on the carpet, where he had thrown her, crying like a silly kid.

It irritated him. "Go on!" he shouted at last, "you don't care all that much for Joe Bogey! You didn't know him above a couple of days ..."

He wondered why she was not frightened of him; he was frightened of himself, he thought fleetingly of his name going down to posterity: The Monster of Fiery Beacon.

After what seemed a long time she quietened down, sat up, mopped her face with a grubby handkerchief and wrapped her arms round her knees once more. "I love Joe Bogey, he was kind and sweet, he helped me and made everything seem to be coming all right for me. He was *nice* and I love Pa and Ma Bogey too, like they were my own family, only much more." She gave a deep, shuddering, after-crying sigh: "This will kill them when they know. Haven't they enough trouble, poor dears?"

It was an extreme anti-climax when W. Sledge remarked that this information would teach her, if she had been in any doubt, as to what sort of person she was dealing with.

What next?

The north sky had cleared, the sun was shining, it was a lovely evening. W. Sledge's restlessness took over. "Let's go and get summat to eat," he suggested in the absence of any activity whatever on the part of Frances, who simply sat, tears running down her cheeks, absently licking them off her face with the tip of her tongue and sniffing extensively.

"Is Mrs. Bogey back at work?" he asked, and when she didn't reply he repeated the question.

"You're either going to play ball . . . or you're not," he complained. "If you're going away with me you'll want your traps, if not . . . not."

She said: "1 don't know what you think I am, you've just told me you've killed your best friend and then you think I'm going to come away with you. What's the matter with you?"

Since he didn't answer she answered. for him: "There's too many things the matter with you to be able to answer that one, isn't there? I'm frightened of you, all right, I'm terribly, terribly frightened of you . . ."

He turned his head and looked at her with some curiosity.

". . . and yet, on the other hand, I'm not."

"Why not?"

"Why not?" she repeated, to mark time, "why not?"

"*Why not?*" he shouted, adding: "Damn you!"

"Because," she began slowly and thoughtfully, "you're not all that bad; when we met in the coffee bar, I thought you were nice and those things I thought were nice, still are . . . nice."

"What, for instance?"

"I mean . . . you do look at a girl as though she was a person and not *only* a sex-pot and . . ."

"Go on . . ."

"And it was quite decent of you to take me out in your car, even though you did try to scare me, and succeeded. And you didn't only take me out for sheer . . . sheer sex."

"Oh, didn't I? You're wrong there, you clever little tick. I did, but I changed my mind, remembering I had a job on that night."

"Well, anyway," she returned, looking up blandly at the ceiling, "anyway . . . it's a lovely evening, let's go there again . . . to Maidenhead, the river will be nice tonight . . ."

Anyone with more imagination might have seen a red warning light, flickering on and off, somewhere around the top of her head. As it was, W. Sledge only very faintly seemed to smell burning. He swung his legs off the arm of the sofa and sat with his elbows on his knees, looking at her thoughtfully but not really thinking.

"Why not?" she argued. "The worst of the rush-hour will be over, we can go down the M4, in your new car." Pause. "How about it?"

He wanted to change his clothes, vain always as to his appearance, and the final result would have been better without the topping of thick black hair, as all his clothes had been chosen to complement the red hair. He changed his snazzi-pants to tight black corduroys and put on his dark glasses.

She gave him a quick glance over: "You'll do," she threw off casually, and drew in tightly the belt round the middle of her short striped fun-fur coat, so tightly that she was short of breath, but in any case, she could scarcely breathe for excitement and, yes, fear.

As they drew away from the parking lot and stopped to allow a car to pass in front of them before emerging on to the road she gave a gasp: it was an open MG and in it was Silas d'Ambrose, wearing his deerstalker hat. They followed him towards the main road but before reaching it he turned off abruptly to the left, up an entirely irrelevant road.

"See who that was?" W. Sledge asked.

"No," she said blankly, "no."

"It was your friend from the pizza bar, your boss."

"Rubbish! You can't see properly in those ridiculous glasses!"

CHAPTER XIII

Mrs. Bogey's fingers were trembling as she put them to her lips. "No, Mr. d'Ambrose, she hasn't come back. I ... we ... we don't know where she is, really we don't, any more than we know where Joe is. This is a terrible state of affairs we've got ourselves into! I feel if only I hadn't stayed away those last two days; all went well till those two days I stayed over; if only I'd come back when I intended to!"

Silas said: "And I'm perfectly sure that when I say your boy's best friend is a homicidal maniac it sounds nonsense to you. But as I see it, Mrs. Bogey, there has to come a moment in the career of any, let's say, homicidal maniac (even if I'm wrong) when he has to start, something happens to tip it off. Nobody's told me anything, I've had to guess most of what I know and the police aren't giving away anything; I've been to see them and told them all I've guessed about Sledge but they're waiting for us to give ourselves away and tell a whole lot more, about Joe, too!"

"Everything happened at once!" Mrs. Bogey wept, "and it's all because I stayed away. If I hadn't been away that night, our Joe would never have brought the girl home ... there wouldn't have been room. He only wanted to make use of my bedroom for that one night ..."

"The girl being here may not have had much to do with anything, she was just an added complication, but the point was, she wouldn't have come to Fiery Beacon at all if it hadn't been that she met Sledge in the morning, the first day of her so-called adventure."

"The only thing I can suggest, Mr. d'Ambrose, is that you go and see the Sledge parents, they're on the eighth floor front, they may know somethink. You may even find Sledgey there ... oh, sorry, I can't help calling him that, it's what Joe always called him."

So the last desperate thing Silas could do was to ask Mrs. Bogey to tell Frances to be sure to ring him, when she came in, *if* she came in and, sadly, she closed the door after him.

"We can't go on like this," she said to her husband after he left.

"Now, don't lose your nerve," Mr. Bogey begged, "or we will be in the soup; it's not like you, dearie; look, your hands are trembling. We've done our best and I can't see as we can do any more. All we've got to do is to stay ... let's say ... deadpan. Just stay deadpan and let it all roll over us!"

"Stay deadpan," Mrs. Bogey repeated firmly as she stared at her own white face in the looking-glass over the radiator.

So down to the eighth floor.

"Who is it?" Mrs. Sledge called nervously through the closed door. He called his name but as she probably would not have the slightest idea who he was he added: "Of the Soho Pizza Bar where your son's friend Joe Bogey works."

She opened the door cautiously and peered out, half a cigarette was protruding from her mouth as fixed-looking as a small piece of overflow pipe. Having looked him over she opened the door wide enough for him to be able to pass through without much difficulty, then snapped it shut. She was wearing rollers in her hair and had evidently been reading a woman's magazine, as she was still holding it in her hand.

She asked him into the living-room, explained that her husband was not home from work, then said she felt sure he had come about their son Winston. And without waiting for any reply she went on that they really did disown Winston, he was over twenty-one now and they no longer had any responsibility for him. Why did people bother to call? Didn't they understand, Winston was a grown man now and they couldn't influence him one way or another?

Like a mindless goldfish, Silas opened and shut his mouth several times without succeeding in saying anything.

"Sit down, Mr. Er," she invited, sitting down herself and lighting another cigarette from the stub. "Winston has been more than a disappointment to me and my husband, he was a lovely kid, I must say that for him, the loveliest kid you ever saw! People used to stop me in the street and say: 'Oh, what a lovely kid!' And then, and then ..." for the first time she faltered, "but you wouldn't understand, not being a mother. It was as though ... it was like he was going rotten before my eyes, my *very* eyes! It seemed even before I could turn round, he'd changed from this lovely kid to a long, lanky boy, always up to somethink I knew nothink about, off

on his own, up to I'd no idear what! My husband told me to go along and
see his headmaster and I did. 'Adolescence, Mrs. Sledge, nothink to worry
about,' says he, 'it's just somethink you parents and us schoolteachers have
to put up with,' says he . . . and a whole lot of crap about our Winston
'finding himself.' It's like he hates us now, whenever he comes home, and
that's not often, he's so, so lar-di-dar . . . makes you sick . . ."

"Mrs. Sledge," Silas at last managed to, as it were, get his foot in the
door, like someone trying to sell encyclopaedias, and when she paused
for a fleeting second he could not collect his thoughts in time to start
off instantly and very nearly missed his chance. "Joe Bogey!" he snapped.
just in time.

"What about him?"

"Where is he?"

"How should I know?"

"Have the police been here?"

"Yes."

"What about?"

"Asking me, or trying to ask me, questions about Winston. They asked
if I knew he had a flat in this block under another name. 'Know,' I said,
'I know nothink at all!' It gave me a turn, though, the nerve of it! And
all along he's been saying he lived in Colindale with two other chaps."

And then Mrs. Sledge stopped pulling at her cigarette and her head
almost fell forward on her chest as she murmured, "They were on about
an Indian girl our Winston's supposed to have been keeping as a mistress,
she threw herself down it seems . . . outside . . ." she jerked her head in
wordless explanation.

Silas paused out of consideration for her feelings but finally said it
was Joe Bogey he was worried about. She told him that Joe Bogey had
always been a friend of Winston, ever since they were kids, she didn't
know where he was or anything about him, except his parents lived on
the top floor front; never had, he was just a friend.

Then Silas asked for the number of the flat Winston had taken and she
said she didn't know but the name was Ledge. "That's Winston all over,"
she couldn't help a slight smile, "cunning like a fox, a near-lie is always
better than a great big one, that's what he said to me once. I must say
he's got somethink there, a big whopping lie . . . I mean to say . . . people
don't believe you, do they? But a near-lie . . . oh yes, he's a foxy one, that!"

Since he had managed to get some information out of her, from sheer courtesy Silas let her work it all out of herself and when she was becoming spent from solid talking, he left.

And it so happened that he called at the seventeenth floor north side flat a short time before W. Sledge returned from his abortive visit to Madame Joan. Just at the moment Frances had turned on the bath water for a fine, full hot bath, and did not hear knock or bell. He rang and knocked and it was clear, he thought, that no live person was in the flat who wanted to answer the door, but there could well be a dead one or ones.

There was nothing more to do about it but to go to the police, even though he was not hopeful, and discuss with them his fears. As usual they were deadly noncommittal.

After that it was time to return to the pizza bar to see that the evening staff were there present and correct, but he felt impelled to call, once again, at the Bogeys' flat, to see if Frances had returned. He knew how irresponsible she could be but he optimistically believed she knew enough not to allow herself to be alone with Sledge.

Mrs. Bogey was again kind and, this time, very understanding. "I know just how you're feeling about Frances," she murmured sympathetically, "we feel that way ourselves, we've grown very fond of that girl, Mr. d'Ambrose. Mind you, she likes to dramatise things, I know that full well, but she'll settle down."

He was amazed. Joe missing and now, possibly, Frances, and Mrs. Bogey no more perturbed than if they were simply late home. He wondered if, perhaps, Mrs. Bogey's misfortune with her husband had been so great that she put up a huge resistance to any further disasters. It was the only explanation he could think up.

Moodily he descended in the lift and went across to his car, climbed in, started up and drove off the parking lot, turning right, towards the King's Road.

A white Rover 2000 was coming out of the parking lot at the back of Fiery Beacon and waited for him to pass. He would never have any idea why he looked at it again in his driving mirror, he certainly did not do it thinkingly.

Sheer excitement caused an extraordinary shrinking feeling inside his clothes, he felt tiny, suddenly, and hardly able to hold on to the steering wheel, but as they neared the King's Road he pulled himself together, remembered to switch on his indicator, turned briskly to the left, into a side street, instantly reversed faster than he would have thought possible, and out again to follow the Rover, left in the King's Road and on . . . and on . . . and on.

Go west, young man.

Till you get to the Hammersmith flyover.

And on.

And on, keeping right as you mount the glorious sweep skyward, over the houses and factory roofs at seventy-five miles an hour . . .

Seventy miles an hour being the limit at that time on the M4, the white Rover took wing and went much faster where the road narrows beyond Slough and the traffic thins out but he did not lose sight of it . . . just.

END OF MOTORWAY 1 MILE.

He could have caught up now but he didn't. Keeping his distance he followed, round the roundabout, along the straight towards Henley . . . a sharp turn to the right, again to the left, across a common and then he really lost sight of it in the narrow country lane that all motorways seem to end in, with people trying to drive far too fast because they have caught the habit on the motorway but having to crawl behind a stream of other crawling cars. Thus he slid past the entrance to the hotel car-park by the river, seeing the white Rover *only just* as it stopped, choosing a parking place. He shot over the bridge still too fast, then, in the little country riverside town, stopped and thought. It would be foolish to return and park in the same hotel car-park but he thought of a better plan. He reversed the MG again and drove slowly back over the river; looking left he saw the Rover parked, saw both doors open and out of the nearside door he saw Frances's lovely legs. He slid slowly past looking for somewhere to leave his car along the road beyond the hotel; it was not easy but a young woman was cutting a hedge in front of a bungalow in the evening sunshine and very charmingly Silas asked if he might leave his car.

"How long?"

"Could I possibly . . . until I've dined?"

"Well, yes . . ." she hesitated, "but my husband will be home about ten."

Silas was almost effusive, he would take it away long before then. But he was not at all sure that he would, as he walked back towards the hotel. What if they were there for the night?

"You're very quiet, love," W. Sledge remarked. "What'll you have? You're not much company tonight, I must say!"

"All right, I'll have a créme-de-menthe, on the rocks, a big one."

She took a seat by the bar window overlooking the river and presently he carried the drink across to her. "On an empty stomach," he remarked, "this should do you good!"

She took a big gulp of it, without raising her glass to him, avoiding his look. "I'm shaking inside."

"Good!"

"Don't get me wrong, it's your sadism, you like scaring the life out of me, don't you!"

But the créme-de-menthe, followed by another, didn't really lighten the atmosphere, which was heavy and depressing. She was dreamy, very unlike her too-communicative self. They chose what they were going to eat from the menu and when it was ready they went into the dining room. The drink made her even more morose.

"You're like a broody hen," he complained. "What's up?"

"I'm thinking."

"About us, I hope. Oh, it's going to be marvellous, kid! Marvellous! A breath of fresh air and getting away from it all!"

She hardly touched her food, pushing aside most of the expensive meal, at which he complained bitterly, but enjoyed his own meal.

With the coffee he begged her to "perk up." "Are you feeling all right?" he added, peering closely at her. Her face was extremely pale and her eyes appeared to have enlarged; her hands were trembling. She said she was feeling sick and that was something with which he could sympathise.

"It's your nerves," he said reassuringly, "me too, get that badly sometimes."

His kindness was unendurable; she turned away, ashy.

She got up and ran from the table, she left her handbag on the floor, under her chair. Intentionally.

Silas, having followed them thus far, could not bear to lose sight of them. Nor could he bear to leave his pizza bar for long without his own supervision. He felt he had to have a telephone call to Mrs. James Trelawny telling her he was unavoidably held up but would be back "at any moment," which threat would keep them, as he called it, "on their toes." There was nothing Mrs. James Trelawny liked better than to be left in charge of the pizza bar; but Silas thought it was bad for the bar's image, her presence giving it more than a taint of an English seaside tea-room.

Observing now that his couple were dining together by candlelight and that the evening was fading into twilight, he slipped out and over the bridge into the main street, where he hurried the length and back on the other side, without seeing a public telephone.

He went to the bar and fortified himself with two glasses of stout and rum and a packet of potato crisps.

He sat brooding as he smoked the last but one of his Balkan Sobranie: he very much loved his Frances Smith, and for the first time in his life thought he had met a girl whom he wanted to marry, and by that he meant a virgin and a girl who would remain faithful to him.

He had judged Frances to be both these things but tonight he was shaken; he didn't mind her unpredictability but he had to satisfy himself that it was not sexual.

So he waited in some disgust because he felt like some paid private sleuth, to see if they had booked a room in the hotel or whether they would drive back to town and retire together into the Ledge flat in Fiery Beacon. If they did either of those things the affair between Frances and himself was at an end; an unfaithful wife was one of the things which, he told himself, he would not put up with. And with the second stout and rum he was filled with a stubborn Victorian righteousness.

Lurking outside the dining-room he saw the waiter taking coffee to their table, then he went out to the car-park and concealed himself behind a still brown beech hedge with its pointed buds on the verge of explosion, running between the car-park and the narrow strip of lawn.

Just below the hotel, half of the river was diverted into a long, shallow weir; it was part of the hotel's charm that the sound of this weir was constantly present, soft or loud according to the pressure of water. At the moment it was very loud indeed and he realised that he would not hear a word they spoke when they came out, if they did come out.

Silas did not have to wait so very long, out they both came, evidently having dined without enjoyment. It was almost dark now, the only light being from the windows of the hotel, all except the candlelit dining-room windows which looked over the river in the front and not over the car-park.

W. Sledge found the key in his pocket and opened the door of his car, climbed in and leaned forward to release the lock on the passenger's side. She opened the door and shouted so that he could hear above the sound of the weir: "Oh Sledgey, I've left my bag . . . under the seat I sat in at dinner!"

Sulkily but always the gent, he got out and as he walked back to the hotel entrance she nipped round to the driver's seat. By now Silas was too fascinated to care whether or not she saw his white face peering through the newly sprouting beech hedge or not. He had to see what she was doing.

And it was this: she was fumbling with something beneath the steering wheel, which, from his position, he could not see but which he knew to be the padded flap of the glove locker; he saw her right arm tugging something; it was the wire handle of the bonnet catch, in a Rover cunningly concealed in the glove compartment which could be locked with the engine key, against anyone interfering with the engine.

If there had been no noise from the weir he would have heard the click of the bonnet catch released and the glove locker snapped shut. For some reason she was going to open the bonnet. She came round to the front, the bonnet being within two feet or so of the hedge, and putting her fingers under the bonnet edge she ran them along until she felt the second safety catch. She released this, too. She raised the bonnet an inch or so to make sure it was free, then replaced it very gently so that the catch would not re-engage.

She then went across the drive to meet Sledge as he came out of the hotel, carrying her handbag; she took it from him and they stood there, she talking earnestly whilst Silas pulled himself together. He was going to be left out of this if he wasn't careful. He ran to the end of the hedge, climbing over a two-bar fence, past some outbuildings and out into the road. He hurried along to where he had left his MG. Before climbing in and starting up the engine he called to the young woman, whom he could see outlined against a light in a downstairs room.

"Thanks!"

She waved.

He started up his car, backed out into the road and sat, side lights on (for it was darkening), engine being gently revved up, waiting for the Rover. It seemed a very long time coming and when it came, what was he going to do? Was he simply going to lean out and shout: "Look out for your bonnet catches, they're undone!" and drive off madly? Whatever it was he had to do it; apart from his anxiety about his girl-friend there were other people to consider; the car was in no condition to go on to the Motorway, or any other highway.

The first large white car that approached was not the Rover, and he had to apologise for waving it down. But finally he saw it coming, very slowly because it had not had time to get into a high gear; this time he took no chances, he jumped out of his own car and stood in the middle of the road.

Sledge was in a towering temper, he leaned out shouting, recognised Silas immediately and threatened him with instant annihilation if he didn't move. He kept his hand pressed on the horn and moved forward so that Silas had to jump clear and away and there was no possible chance of the driver hearing what Silas was shouting.

But one thing was for sure—she was not in the car, the driver was alone.

Silas drove his car into the hedge, not caring this time where he left it, and ran back to the hotel.

The mixture of stout and rum and shock were not conducive to mental alertness and it was only as he was running hotel wards that he realised that if he telephoned to the police he would be asked his name or that if he didn't, the call giving them the lethal information could easily be traced. He would find Frances first, drive her to a call-box and insist that she make her own call. It was only right that her irresponsible behaviour should be brought home to her. Her action was parallel with that of the man who, wishing to kill a single enemy, plants a bomb in a crowded plane.

"Where's that girl?" he shouted to the hall porter.

"What girl, sir?"

"The girl, the girl . . . she's wearing a striped fur coat. She was standing out here a few minutes ago. She was with a chap . . ."

"Yes, sir, I know the one you mean. I've no idea where she is!"

He tore back to his car, he backed it out of the hedge, after a few trial attempts, it skidded on the muddy grass, but after several minutes had flipped past, he was free. Then he had to drive some hundred yards to find a suitable place to turn.

He had to turn, he seemed always to be turning—

He drove past the hotel and into the street of the little town, looking once again for a telephone box he might have missed. He still could not see one. He stopped the car, shouting at the first person he saw: "Telephone box?" It was a foreigner, of course, a stranger in these parts; it always was. He stopped again beside two schoolgirls, flopping along the pavement licking ice-cream cornets. When they got the message they burst into uncontrollable giggles about Silas's hat, though he was not to know this was the cause of their merriment. They finally managed to tell him that there was a telephone box in the council houses, round to the right, first left, he couldn't miss it. He could miss it and did. He tried again and found it. There were about four boys crammed inside, he pulled them out, the dial was sticky, the atmosphere was solid with cigarette smoke, they were making faces at him through the glass.

Nine, nine, nine.

"There is a white Rover 2000 making for the M4. Both the bonnet catches are undone. It must be stopped before the Motorway. Sorry, I don't know the number." Gently he replaced the receiver and made a face at the jeering boys that greatly outdid their own for sheer ugliness.

Back at the hotel he insisted to the hall porter that he *must* know where the girl in the striped fur coat was and the hall porter was quite plaintive in assuring him that he did not. One of the cashiers, however, was helpful. "She asked at the desk if there was a station. Well, the station's closed, actually, but they told her she could get a train easily at Maidenhead. She asked how to get to Maidenhead and someone told her. She said she'd hitch-hike."

"She had her handbag with her," Silas argued, unreasonably irritated, "she could have paid for a cab!"

But now everybody's helpfulness ran out. Nobody knew anything more. He went out on to the now quite dark lawn and walked briskly up and down beside the river. His face cooled, his anxiety cooled. Perhaps it hadn't happened. Or perhaps, if it had happened, the bonnet lid would wobble, perhaps Sledge's attention would be drawn to it as he drove, inevitably not fast, towards the M4. Perhaps it was all such stuff as nightmares are made on . . . like Joe Bogey being murdered by his friend.

Silas looked himself over, he appeared the same, from this viewpoint but sometimes life was so fantastic, it made you wonder. Deflated, he walked back to the MG, climbed in and drove away from the riverside hotel.

He was caught in the usual procession of cars and the driving was so monotonous he was near enough having stopped thinking by the time he went round the roundabout and on to the Motorway. He pressed down the accelerator with that recurring pleasure one has on starting along a Motorway, enjoying the delight of the engine to be released from the frustration of being driven along a narrow country lane.

It had happened all right, within a mile of the start. As he rounded the first bend the flashing lights slowed him down and finally he was waved to a stop.

Cars were still rushing past along the opposite carriage-way.

He drew on to the hard. He got out of the MG and sat down on the grass verge, he didn't want to look at the disorder or see what the floodlighting revealed, the aftermath: he buried his face in his hands.

The eastward lane, to London, was entirely blocked, though the westward lane still seemed free of trouble. Cars coming westward had to stop and crowds of people were getting out. "It won't be long," he heard them saying, and someone in the know said "A Rover is trapped under a pantechnicon and the van has toppled over."

Within half an hour the furniture van had been righted with two lorry cranes, and towed away, the smashed Rover had been removed, too, topless. The ambulances had driven away and the Motorway was clear. The highway maintenance men with huge brushes, were clearing glass from the surface of the roadway. Policemen were taking down statements from a number of witnesses. Another half-hour and it was all over. Silas rose stiffly and went towards his car.

"What happened, Officer?" he said to a policeman who was making his way to his motorcycle.

"Seems the poor blighter forgot to put his bonnet flap down proper. It flew open against his windscreen and he ran straight into the back of a big van at around eighty."

"Is he killed?"

"What do you expect? Decapitated," the policeman said tightly. "But it's lucky he didn't swerve over the centre; there'd have been slaughter, absolute bloody slaughter. Two chaps in the furniture van are not badly hurt. Could have been a lot worse."

Silas drove back at not more than forty miles an hour.

CHAPTER XIV

It was after midnight when Frances stumbled out of the taxi from Paddington, gave the driver a pound note without waiting for the change, and took the lift up to the Bogeys' flat. Her eyes and nose were running, she had a terrible headache, she felt vilely sick because créme-de-menthe on the rocks does not make a good apéritif. She could not get the key into the lock the right way up but Mrs. Bogey, still up and sitting with her husband, came and opened the door for her, in her dressing-gown.

Hysterically Frances threw her arms round Mrs. Bogey's neck, weeping in great gasps.

Thin cries of distress came from Pa Bogey's room, he wanted to know what was happening.

Frances stood in the hall and shouted everything out wildly. "I fixed the Rover," she screamed. Shocked, Mrs. Bogey tried to calm her, pulling her into Mr. Bogey's room where Frances flung herself across his bed and wept wildly. "I'm partly drunk!" she kept saying.

Tea was the best remedy; Mrs. Bogey hastened to get it whilst Mr. Bogey kept a feeble hand on Frances's head and gently patted it to reassure her.

When they had finally persuaded her to have some tea their calm acceptance of her condition had its effect, she subsided into occasional huge shuddering sobs.

"What do you say you did, dear?"

"The only thing I could think of, Mrs. Bogey."

"And what was that, dear, Dad and I don't quite understand."

"A Rover, you see. A friend of my father nearly had a ghastly accident in his, only he was only going slowly. They forgot when he filled up with petrol and oil, they forgot to shut the bonnet properly and it flew up and shattered his windscreen, but as he was going fairly slowly, it didn't do much harm. He just stopped very quickly, he said he'd have been killed if he'd been going fast. You see, Sledge went too fast, he did it to frighten

150

me. But it may not have worked with him, either, there's a long slow narrow country lane before you get to the Motorway, you can't drive fast along it and maybe he's run into a hedge or . . . or anything. But the thing is he'll know I did it, sure to! I had a frightful row with him. You see, he locked me up in his bathroom and I really think he was going to starve me to death; however, he thought he'd killed me and was scared stiff till I shouted."

"I don't understand, dear."

"I don't suppose you can, Mrs. Bogey, nobody could understand Sledge. Once he'd killed one person he doesn't care who he kills now. The woman in Kensington, probably the Indian girl, who knows, and I'm sure, Mrs. Bogey, I'm sure he's killed Joe, he practically told me so and . . . he must have . . . because where is Joe?"

Mr. and Mrs. Bogey exchanged long, as they say, cool looks.

"I know he's mad, anyone who knows Sledge would know he's mad but if he were locked up and doctors and psychiatrists examined him . . . they wouldn't say he was mad, or unfit to plead . . . well, he isn't unfit to plead, but he's mad all the same. And he sounds so sane, until he's, what? Thwarted? It was outside that hotel, on the river, I went out to dinner there with him because we'd been before and I was going to . . . to do what I did . . . but I had to pretend, first, that I was going away with him. I know he was going to kill me next when I said I wouldn't dream of going away with him. So I had dinner, only I spoilt it all by having about four crème-de-menthes on the rocks first and I felt so sick and awful. I fixed the car all right but outside the hotel we had a row, I said I wasn't going away after all and it was better to part now but instead of talking it over calmly as I'd planned we had this screaming abuse and . . . oh, it was awful, only the ghastly noise from the weir made it not as bad as it might have been to everyone listening. People might have come rushing out to see who was going to kill who. I dashed back into the hotel and just sat in the loo crying and waiting till he'd gone and for a long time after."

"And did he go?"

She nodded. "He was in a furious temper, I watched him drive off—as a matter of fact!"

Mrs. Bogey was anxious to get her out of Mr. Bogey's room now; it was her only ambition at the moment and she achieved her aim after quite a lot more trouble.

"Well, dear?" she said when she had edged Frances into the room in which she was sleeping, "I'm sorry, I'm so very sorry you've had all this worry about Joe. We couldn't tell you because, as Dad says, the fewer people knew the better. We got him out to Ireland."

Frances's mouth almost fell open.

"But how?"

"You may well ask. That evening I came back, after you'd gone to bed I put on my headscarf and coat and crept in to your room to get a few clothes for Joe and ... Oh, my dear, you've no idea; never mention it to his Dad, he did what he hated to do, he begged Joe to go; Dad says he played on Joe's pity for him but even so, what's it matter? It's not a crime to be sorry for your crippled father, is it? Dad says, he says: 'Please go to your sister, Joe, for my sake,' and he went but not willingly; I took most of our savings and I went with him and sat with him at the airport, half the day, until a seat on a plane to Dublin turned up." Mrs. Bogey could not resist a smile: "I waited till it took off! You thought I was back at work, didn't you? Well, there you are. Any comment?"

"Oh my God, no!" Frances moaned.

Finally Mrs. Bogey gave Frances two tranquilliser pills she had kept for emergencies and when she was sure she was asleep she crept into her husband's bedroom, closing the door. "I've told her. Oh love! If she's managed to finish off Sledge what a let-out for us all! Am I wicked?"

Mr. Bogey was big-eyed but pale with shock and excitement, he could not answer.

And at the end of the eight a.m. news on the radio: "... eastward-bound traffic lane of the M4 near Maidenhead was blocked for an hour last night ... driver of a car was killed, the police think the accident was due to the flying up of the bonnet lid whilst travelling at a fast speed ..."

"Amen and thank God," Mr. Bogey said.

"I must show her Joe's letter ..." Mrs. Bogey said.

It read:

Ballyhoola, Megimmick, Eire.

Dear Mum and Dad,

Sis says I must write and tell you that things are going well, even (she says), if I don't deserve it. A friend of Sis's husband has this caff and

Mick had a talk with him about turning it into a pizza bar; so now I've given up digging what they call "taties" and am helping him to fit out this bar which he *wants me to run*. Sis says it'll go like a bomb, being as it's something quite new in Ballyhoola and what it needs. I only hope things are not too bad with you and you're not being worried by anything Sledge-wise.

And Sis says I am to say I'm sorry; she says it's not enough being sorry, I must say it. So here goes.

I'm sorry, Mum and Dad, and I will do my very best to show you I am by . . . oh well, I will.

From your loving and turned-over-a-new-leaf

Joe

Love to Frances Smith.

Frances cried yet again when she had read it. "So you hustled him away to his sister; why didn't you tell me, Mrs. Bogey?"

"Dad and I thought best not to tell anyone, we gave him the money and told him to get out quick, it seemed the best we could do, whilst expecting the worst. Even if it means Dad may never see Joe again."

A wraith, or shadow of her former self, utterly subdued, dressed herself none too carefully and left the Bogeys' flat for "work."

Silas was frowning, giving a visible demonstration of the Wrath of God in which he no longer believed but fervently wished he did, or thought he did. Though Justice had been done to Sledge, via Frances Smith, ought not Justice to be meted out to Frances Smith too?

He was sure it ought. She had shocked him so profoundly that he felt quite unable to cope with her and uncertain of himself; he only hoped his frown would show her in some small measure how he felt.

She put up a very good appearance of nonchalance, looking rather like a dirty young cat who had been out all night, scrapping, mating, screaming, getting soaked with rain . . . but bravely putting a good face on it, like Mehitabel:

"Hell's Bells,
I'm still a lady!"

"Well, what's the matter with *you?*" she had the extraordinary impertinence to ask.

He gave a short and what he hoped was a bitter bark of non-laughter. "You behave just any old how, don't you? You assume, you actually assume that everything is going your way ..."

She stood directly in front of him.

"What's the matter?"

Silas was unnerved by the presence of Mrs. James Trelawny who, he knew, was lurking behind the curtain endeavouring to hear everything.

He said: "You thought I was going to let you go off with Sledge to some hypothetical interview with the missing Joe? No, you didn't think at all, did you? It never occurred to you I might wonder ... it never occurred to you I might follow you, even down to the hotel by the river. Just for once, chance helped, or perhaps it was simply using my eyes because you didn't see me pass the end of the road as you were waiting to leave Fiery Beacon in the Rover, did you? But I saw you through the driving mirror."

"Well, so what? Whether you were very clever and saw it all, or not, what does it matter? It happened and you must agree, it's a let-out for Sledge!"

But Frances did, in fact, look abashed, she stared down at the square, clumsy toes of her shoes. Finally she raised her head and said: "You saw the lot, then?"

"Yes, and I rang the police, but too much time had passed for my warning to be of any use. Do you realise how criminally irresponsible you are, you might have involved many, or even one other person, in the so-called accident?"

"I do," she agreed, "and I'm sorry about that, terribly!"

"Sorry!" he practically shouted.

"What more can I say? Are you going to sack me, then?" There was a long pause.

"It's marrying I'm thinking about; you don't realise, do you, that I have some natural aversion ..." and he did in fact lower his voice to a whisper, "... to having a murderess as a wife?"

Then her head really hung, like a broken flower, he thought, or a snowdrop.

"But as a pizza-maker, I suppose, you'll do, as there's nobody else available."

"That hurts!" she said.

He turned away, picking up the newspaper, sitting down and putting his feet on a vacant chair, taking out his packet of Balkan Sobranies and lighting one.

She went through the curtain and hung up her coat on one of the hooks. She was tying the string of her apron behind her back, or trying to and failing because of the tears pouring down, when Mrs. James Trelawny came out of the scullery and, taking the strings from her, tied the apron for her.

She clicked her tongue in sympathy. "I don't know what you've done, dear, I've never seen him so angry!"

Madame Joan had finished her breakfast but continued to sit at the table, engrossed by the tea leaves she saw in her empty cup. Her daughter briskly cleared away everything and washed them up. Then she returned to the table for the cup and found her mother staring down at the tiger's tooth which she was holding in the palm of her hand.

"Whatever's that?" the daughter exclaimed, "it looks a nasty thing!"

"Do you think so? I like it very much. I've inherited it."

"Who from?"

"That young man."

"Which one?"

"He had a lot of very red hair. It went black. He's dead."

"Oh, I'm sorry," her daughter answered absently; she had finished washing up the breakfast things and was now looking at herself in a mirror over the sink. "What did he die of?" she asked absently.

"How should I know?" her mother snapped.

Joan Fleming (1908–1980) was a British author of more than thirty crime and thriller novels. She was born in Lancashire, England, and educated at the City Literary Institute and the University of Lausanne in Switzerland. The British Crime Writers' Association twice awarded her with its prestigious Gold Dagger award for best crime novel of the year, once in 1962 for *When I Grow Rich*, and again in 1970 for *Young Man, I Think You're Dying*.